I'm fascinated by Renée Sarojini Saklikar's ongoing and expansive lyric assemblage, the multiple trade books across her The Heart of This Journey Bears All Patterns. This is a project that should be revered and studied in the same breath as bpNichol's *Martyrology*, Robert Kroetsch's *Completed Field Notes* and Dennis Cooley's *love in a dry land*. Saklikar has clearly absorbed and understood the myriad traditions of the long poem, and furthers the structures into wildly unexpected places; pushing the boundaries of what writing can do, and the formal possibilities of what bpNichol termed a "poem as long as a life."

—rob mclennan

Bramah and the Beggar Boy takes us into a near-future apocalyptic world on an odyssey of our time. Like Melville's great whaling story, Saklikar's marvelous tale rivets us with mind-blowing insights into the destructive forces at work right now in our capitalist world and how we might resist and overcome them. It's a page-turner.

—Meredith Quartermain

With *Bramah and the Beggar Boy*, Renée Sarojini Saklikar has resurrected the epic poem for the Anthropocene, merged it with the visionary qualities of speculative fiction, and woven diasporic threads into a new and necessary act of world making. The future was such a long time ago—but maybe it's not over yet. Throw the dice. Jump the fence. Cross the threshold. The carmen perpetuum, the continuous song of THOT J BAP has begun. Only beauty unfolds from here.

—Stephen Collis

THE HEART of THIS JOURNEY · BEARS ALL PATTERNS ·

THOT J BAP

BRAMAH and the BEGGAR BOY

Renée Sarojini Saklikar

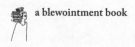

a blewointment book

NIGHTWOOD EDITIONS

2021

Nightwood Editions
P.O. Box 1779
Gibsons, BC VON 1VO
Canada
www.nightwoodeditions.com

COVER DESIGN: Topshelf Creative
COVER ART: Nadina Tandy
TYPOGRAPHY: Carleton Wilson
ILLUSTRATIONS: Line drawings by the author; pine cone and microscope images
(pp. 18, 84, 93) from Wikimedia Commons

Nightwood Editions acknowledges the support of the Canada Council for the Arts, the Government of Canada, and the Province of British Columbia through the BC Arts Council.

This book has been produced on 100% post-consumer recycled, ancient-forest-free paper, processed chlorine-free and printed with vegetable-based dyes.

Printed and bound in Canada.

LIBRARY AND ARCHIVES CANADA CATALOGUING IN PUBLICATION

Title: Bramah and the beggar boy / Renée Sarojini Saklikar.
Names: Saklikar, Renée Sarojini, author.
Description: Poems.
Identifiers: Canadiana (print) 20210159022 | Canadiana (ebook) 20210159065 |
ISBN 9780889714021 (softcover) | ISBN 9780889714038 (HTML)
Classification: LCC PS8637.A52 B73 2021 | DDC C811/.6—dc23

Let all evil die and the good endure

CONTENTS

PART ONE

Arrival at the Gate of the Winter Portal

The Adventures of Bramah and the Beggar Boy

The Parchment Scroll

The Adventures of Bramah and the Beggar Boy Continued

PART TWO

Abigail Discovered

Abigail and Aunty Agatha at the Farm

The Adventures of Abigail

Abigail and Bartholomew

From Migrant Camps to the Stone Marker

At the Gate of the Unlucky

WELCOME TO THE WORLD OF THOT J BAP

released into this fractured world of woe,
this story, messenger, steady and slow

your eyes to read, as your hands to then turn
each page a portal: welcoming return

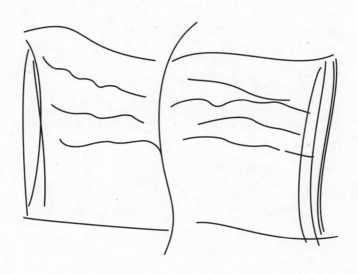

INTRODUCTION

One afternoon, in an old house in an abandoned village on the outskirts of Perimeter, in the place they call Pacifica, Bramah and the Beggar Boy find fragments of an ancient text in an oak box. Hunched over scraps of parchment and broken computer disks, they blow the dust off a cover, and so our story begins.

Steeped in the tradition of fairy tales, The Heart of This Journey Bears All Patterns (THOT J BAP) features a world in which a small band of resisters and survivors meet heartbreak and destruction with rhymes and resourceful skills such as soap and glass making, as well as a belief in the supernatural. Many things happen—some good, but mostly bad—including five eco-catastrophes and a viral bio-contagion. Shape-shifting in and out of it all is the nimble Bramah, a female locksmith, part-human, part-goddess—brown, brave and beautiful.

This is a world governed by climate change and an all-powerful Consortium. Planet Earth is on the verge of a Shift-Tilt and the changes of the seasons are themselves portals to time travel. Alas, even the seasons are mostly controlled by Consortium. Yet, as is so often the case, the powerful can't always stop the hands of fate and the choices humans make. Throughout this poem, we hear the chants of Beggar Boys and Sword Girls as they sing, *Un coup de dés jamais n'abolira le hasard* (a throw of the dice will never abolish chance). The chants and rhymes are a subversive means of communication, foreshadowing events or calling on the help of our hero, Bramah.

Inspired by the tradition of epic sagas, and influenced by poems such as Homer's *Odyssey*, ancient Vedic texts such as the *Mahabharata*, as well as *The Arabian Nights*, the world of THOT J BAP eagerly awaits you.

CHARACTERS

Bramah: an English/Indian (South Asian) locksmith who is a demi-god and hero of the saga. Her motto: *Let all evil die and the good endure.* Bramah works on contract for the Consortium. Rescued by her grandmother after an earthquake, she is unaware of her origins.

The Beggar Boy: Bramah's apprentice. Rescued on one of Bramah's travels. He rarely speaks.

Bramah's grandmother: a storyteller and mendicant known by the Four Women of the Wishing Well. She is a matriarch of the Resistance and adopts orphans.

Dr. A.E. Anderson: born in the year 2020, she is a doctor helping poor village children.

INVESTIGATOR: perennial bad guy. There is one in every age.

Guards of the Fifth Gate: they work for the INVESTIGATOR. Specialists in surveillance.

Consortium: employer of the bad guys.

Rentalsman: Consortium's property agent.

Women of the Wishing Well (Aunty Agatha, Aunty Tabitha, Aunty Maria and Aunty Magda): In this book, we meet **Aunty Maria,** a Seed Saver who works with a group of outlawed scientists. We also meet **Aunty Agatha** and **Aunty Tabitha.** They are mendicant midwives who live over a hundred years.

Abigail: a beggar girl and adopted daughter of Dr. A.E. Anderson.

Bartholomew: scholar, Resistance fighter and lover of Abigail.

Raphael: son of Abigail and Bartholomew.

Beggar Boys: street urchins, displaced orphans who roam Outside Perimeter, often indentured as labourers. Their rhymes and chants, songs and slogans often act as an underground communications system, to which Bramah always pays attention.

Sword Girls: well-bred rebellious women banished by Consortium for misdemeanours, then recruited by Bramah. The Sword Girls are famous for their smarts and weapon skills. They sometimes serve as mercenaries.

The Village Spy and her daughter, **Betty**.

LOCATIONS

Consortium: an integrated global economic and administrative empire controlling all aspects of industry, agriculture and food production.

Perimeter: cities and settlements fortified and controlled by Consortium.

Towers and Gates: this is where guards and agents of Consortium, including the INVESTIGATOR, control who can enter and exit Perimeter.

Gates to the Portals of the Four Seasons: these are found in different locations Outside Perimeter. Although they are controlled by Consortium, if you happen to know the right spells, as Bramah does, the portals can act as departure points for time travel.

Pacifica: a region extending from the western edge of the land mass once known as America.

Cities: these include the Great Cities of Transaction: Toronto, Paris, Baghdad and Ahmedabad.

PART ONE

>>>>>>

>>>>>>

>>>>>>

Arrival at the Gate of the Winter Portal

THAT GATE, THE ORACLE, HER ICY BREATH

Beware increments that gather apace
equinox and solstice shifting in place

O Precession and ecliptic, our Earth
on her axis, tilted and turned, pushed off

course by our actions, her perfect ratio
precision, twenty-three point five and turn

yew berries misshapen, birds drop and fall
fast is our future, the present, all gone

O Precession and ecliptic, our earth
on her axis, tilted and turned, spinning

faster than we could ever imagine
yew berries mutate, their toxin increased

spores, viruses, spreading droplets released
Beware increments that gather apace——

FRAGMENTS OF OLD REPORTS UNVERIFIED

Consortium Assessment: Pacifica Region
in the year of the reign 20XX.

Legal tender done, ice caps melting fast
faster than expected, each paper said

accelerated events, surging tides
extreme conditions overwhelmed systems

low precipitation, extended drought—
wildfires, insect infestations and

water rights abandoned, shortages vast.
faster than expected, each scientist said.

No one left to monitor the changes
effects not well understood, large-scale shifts—

scissors in hand, those beggar children snipped
a thousand pages in exchange for food:

as ordered by the INVESTIGATOR
documents reassembled, then hidden.

CONSORTIUM'S SONG

We can see, in the pulsing places
traces of our mordant graces

Where our tanks grind and crush
scornfully, placate the dust

We can trade and gain and merge,
Bitcoin plus, in case oil's a bust

We give them choice, we find them homes
the finest art, the best designs—

Never mind who doesn't make it
wire us and you can fake it.

We Trace with Scorn

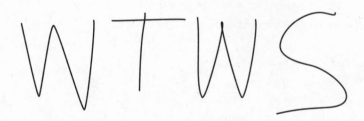

RESISTANCE SONG

At the year's midnight, we sighed, heads bent to—
Perimeter where oracles foretold

colony collapse, our aunties saving
mason bees, small finds in handmade glass jars.

Wildfires in November, ash mixed with ice
our skin dry and cracked, scalps covered in lice,

grey skies unending, snow drought extending
salal leaves withering, their spines snapped in two.

At Tower Juniper, Rentalsman stood
ready to accept payment for shelter.

We bartered our daughters, we sold our boys
WiFi on ration, our androids, no toys:

Toxic Alert on high, we ached for green
who would have thought of us, standing, unseen.

>>>>>>

mind those drones
    they'll break your bones
        hide and sweep,
    duck and swerve
        watch us, learn
    these raindrops burn.

FROM THE WISHING WELL TO PERIMETER'S EDGE

Said the four aunties:
each portal a season, pulling the years
waxing and waning, our joys and our fears.

Said the four winds:
North, East, West, South
corner runners, always best.
    cross your fingers, tell no lies!

Said the River to Perimeter:
Swift currents, sly and deep
you fool with me; I'll make you sleep
    shorter days, longer nights.

Said the City to Consortium:
Secure for us the means, and we'll stay true.

After daybreak, called those Beggar Boys, *Run!*
And their Sword Girls sang, *Every star a sun.*

And together their voices, faint echoes:

Our beehives all empty, our flags, half-mast.
Turn your key, Bramah, and find us at last.

>>>>>>   >>>>>>
♛ ♛ ♛   ♛ ♛ ♛

THE SUMMONS: BRAMAH ON A JOB

Every siren in Perimeter sounded an alarm!

On that day, arrival, although no one
knew who they were, small woman with a boy—

She from around here? asked the settlers, one by one.
Their voices even toned, their eyes, stone cold, gaze
fixed on Bramah's well-oiled leather satchel.

Usurpers, what response might they expect?
Settlers at Perimeter's edge: they wait.

Bramah's slant smile, radiance as a foil,
under her brown hands, hidden from sight

her Pippin File, her keys and her drill, codes
spells and chants to unlock any treasure.

Street beggars, boys with brooms, girls with swords:
from their bruised mouths, parched lips, masks torn away

Until the rains arrive, and we survive—
wash your hands, use your sleeve
trust us now, you'll never have to grieve

At the Fifth Gate, transport drivers lounged:
troop guards to inspect, their hands to scrounge.

Bramah on contract, her face smooth as silk
that Beggar Boy trailing behind,
        that last drop of milk—

VILLAGE WOMEN GOSSIP

at Tower Juniper:

> Our bread set to rise but falling flat,
>   oven door banging, unhinged and broken,
>   all that heat, lost—

at Cedar Cottage:

> Our milk soured,
>   the butter wouldn't set
> and then a black cat ran under the ladder,
>   wood cracked—

at Hemlock Place:

> That dog next door wouldn't stop barking
>   Look! Our keys broken inside their locks, stuck:
> well, Consortium said they'd send someone——

at the Commons, gathered in a circle.
    ——in unison we told Rentalsman:

> Her fingers brown and strong
>   smooth leather satchel
>   her black braid shining
>   Pippin File, drill, tweezers, lock and ghost key
>   pulled one by one, gleaming in the sun,
>   she worked fast, all the while her lips moving:

> *Let all evil die and the good endure*

VIDEO SURVEILLANCE MONITOR, MALFUNCTIONING

As recorded: "Couldn't say how old, but the boy, a ragamuffin for sure, gap-toothed. That hungry smile."

Informer #1: "Of course them keys were stuck, and broke, those locks."

Informer #2: "No one bothered to tell us about any safe."

Informer #3: "Well, if we knew that, then, we'd all be rich, eh—"

Guards of the Fifth Gate: "Someone must have seen something."

>>>>>>

OVERHEARD

Small wiry brown-skinned yet British; sly, too
quick, skilled with lock and key, long black hair
braids touching her leather packsack: tools plus
lasers, all the latest gadgets for openings
no lock that ever met her hands, too tough or sticky.
A thousand scrapes, she'd dodged them all.
One soldier from the Before-Time even called her
K-Low. No one ever knew why. Just laughed.
She collected nicknames, light year to portal:
them hard ones, April, or June: the worst.
In the nick of time, a turner of bad odds
her body on the line of any fire, her cheek scarred
smooth skin though, and the softest lips.
Tattoo on her arm: *Ishmael Joe* and laughed—

AS RECORDED BY SEVERAL UN/NAMED WITNESSES

Front doors locked, we turned: stood, facing the road.
A breath for each forward step, scuffed shoes worn.

In front of us, a woman: long black braid
over her shoulder a leather satchel,

locksmith by trade, her Pippin File, her keys
her pliers, her pick and drill, titanium.

Many called to her and ran to her side.
She held the hand of a small, ragged boy,

his gap-toothed grin——

The Adventures of Bramah and the Beggar Boy

>>>>>>

THEIR FIRST ADVENTURE

The Scraps They Kept: missing pages, cut, torn, stained
The Letters They Took: that red seal, broken, ribbon untied

The Map They Stole: a thousand creases, worn and rough
The People They Met:—Inside and Outside Perimeter—

The Things They Carried: that bronze compass, battered; that gold coin,
    tossed
The Things They Saw: first of two moons, the night Aunty Pandy swept in

The Journeys They Made: by foot, by ship, through beams and holograms
The People They Met: those street-sweeping children, all their songs—

The Things They Carried: masks and hoods—small bars of soap—
The Things They Heard: those Beggar Boys chanting,

Un coup de dés, jamais jamais

THEIR SECOND ADVENTURE

Once inside a Portal, they would divine
streetside or mountains, rivers, oceans, maps
a fist full of soil, their nose to the wind
iterations of this blue-green planet
decades, centuries, era to epoch
in the Before-Time and after: their days
in a café on Rue Mallarmé, that
black book, unlined, cream pages, a few marks
left open with a felt pen inside, no
sign of them, on the wall a painting
rescued from that fire, singed edges framed, hung
over that threshold, carved greetings in wood
golden locket opened from round that neck
that time they met, diving into the wreck.

THEIR THIRD ADVENTURE

Hold my hand and don't let go, said Bramah
The little Beggar Boy kept his head down.

In the year of the reign, these portals deep:

In the year of the reign 2020
In the year of the reign 2001
In the year of the reign 1985
In the year of the reign 1973
In the year of the reign 1968
In the year of the reign 1962
In the year of the reign 1933
In the year of the reign 1945
In the year of the reign 1914
In the year of the reign 1919
In the year of the reign 1848
In the year of the reign 1897
In the year of the reign 1704
In the year of the reign 1715
In the year of the reign 1613
In the year of the reign 1492
In the year of the reign 1381
In the year of the reign 1215
In the year of the reign 762—
And in the time of the Age—
And before—and then further, further, that far future, flung—
The distance between———
And then to return to Pacifica.
Silent, that Beggar Boy took it all in.

THE BEGGAR BOY MEETS BRAMAH'S GRANDMOTHER

When Bramah brought the boy to Grandmother
they both laughed: *Not another one to feed!*
Oh well, said Grandmother, shaking her head.
Come with me boy, you can help carry seeds.

—that Beggar Boy said not a word and looked
    at Grandmother, her warm hands, her unlined skin.
She taught him everyday threshold magic:
the way all doors and gates stored their secrets
the way calendars contained codes
the way dawn and dusk, circles and lines
    might lead to a thousand steps.

One night they walked past that carved portal gate
Grandmother took the boy's hand and shook kernels,
red dawn, sequoia swirls, hard spindle-shaped,
seeds as thin as oatmeal flakes fluttered down.

Two lovers locked in one another's arms.
Gates, doors, locks. Midnight. April. October.
Portals to a very still afternoon.
Electricity and the Inner-Net.
Birds. Stars. Trees. The names of things, rough, smooth, whole.

Ruptures and interruptions.
Tilts and slants.
That game of chess, unending, and the Dead.
The Rani of Jhansi, her lotus flowers.
The city of Ahmedabad, twelve gates opening—

Roses.
Honeybees, their panniers, gold laden.
Green, blue, black, pink. Ombré shades in between.
Rajas and Sutras, hours before dawn.
Cardamom, ginger, turmeric, crushed.

The years: Before to After, sweet. Salty.
Echoes of the S-curve in everything.

English, French, Arabic, Irish.
Gujarati, Latin, Greek: pictograms.
Long yards of Indigenous dialects.
These were unearned, sacred, and Forbidden.

Pottery-painting-prints-jewelry-tattoos.
Weavers, smiths, warriors. Edges and borders.
Thresholds, after-parties, covert ops, slant.
Vast armies on a darkling plain. Empire.

Land masses: geology and shape-shifting.
Glaciers. Earthquakes. Tsunamis and currents.
The town of towns. The Rann of Kutch. Raindrops.
The Lance of Kanana. Mother Lakshmi.
Aunty Maria. Aunty Magda, too.
All the women of the Wishing Well. Winds:
North, South, East, West, circles, squares eroding—

Tundra, shield, meadows. Green hills far away.
Bogs and peat. Granite. Oceans, rivers, tides.

The Moon, her many mistresses, singing:
   layers, fragments, communion and makeup
          adornment, dresses, high heels and barefoot.
            Scheherazade, one thousand tales within——

Perimeter, that Detention Centre:
just Outside, where roving Beggar Boys sang,
Come ye in, airborne, after, masks and hoods,
masks and hoods.
Time.

THE MAP THEY STEAL

For You Who ⬡ May Return, if without soap
barter with Aunty Agatha at the farm.

If in Pacifica, ⬡ retrace your steps: ⬡

    Take the Albion Ferry ⬡, then by foot
    before the airlines shut down all the flights.

THE THINGS THEY TAKE

Bramah:—*those go down first, yeah, before you fum-i-gate*

that Beggar Boy smiles, nods his head, pulls his mask tight
    gloved fingers rip cotton rags, turpentine
    all their finds, dipped, wiped, stored, to be bartered.

Bramah, smiling, her brown hands to the boy's:
a packet of letters, tied up with faded red string:

I did ⬡⬡ miss you, then.
I am resolved to write,
no matt⬡er what hap⬡pens.
Inscription tools and surface material:
I think about ⬡ these a lot.

Discarded letters found in an oak box
Your hand crushing mine, our lips never kissed.

♕ ♕ ♕

GRANDMOTHER'S INSTRUCTION

Later, past midnight, around the campfire
Bramah's grandmother calls everyone in,

closer to the flames. The Beggar Boy sits,
his hands pull on that packet of letters
                his fingers do the reading——
shapes rubbed, upward strokes: dots, crossed *t*s leaning
not even his lips move, not ever, him silent as the night.

⬡

Discarded letters found in an oak box
Your hand crushing mine, our lips never kissed.

⬡

Everyone laughs then, watching the boy's fingers,
and Grandmother says,
    Bramah, next time be sure to search the farmhouse.

VIDEO SURVEILLANCE: INVESTIGATOR'S LOGBOOK

<u>By Order of Consortium:</u> camera numbers defaced.

<u>Locator:</u> Pacifica Region, Outside Perimeter
<u>In the year of the reign 2XXX</u>
<u>Video Surveillance Monitor Status:</u> On

<u>Partial Recording, Retrieved:</u> Farmhouse.

<u>Squadron leader, Guards of the Fifth Gate (~~name~~):</u>

Funny how many of you posted in here.
We was told the lock needed opening fast.

Did you stay with her the whole time, then, eh—
All them cameras we tested worked just fine.

So I guess she just did some spell on them?

BRAMAH AND THE BEGGAR BOY FIND AN OLD OAK BOX

Her long black braid, her locksmith tools, clipped.
His gap-toothed smile, his no-name runners ripped.

What is it? he asked—they lifted the lid—
inside parchment, codes printed on paper
                   fragments—
       a handful of dusty disks
     a book, letters and many other things:

rubbed, held, stolen, ransomed—tied up with string,
brought back, bartered from the Before-Time—when—

Outside Perimeter, the boys chanted:
Right as rain, good as new,

Jumped the fence, you should too—
    Jumped the fence, you should too—

THE LETTER THEY FIND

Dear Future Survivors:

Our only defence against gas, frayed scarves
no mistaking the colour of our skin—

We would search October and April, then—
We would find no traces of doors or gates

or doors only where locks turned, then jammed, eyes
scanned, for re-entry, or bribes, or bodies—

We are sending you this message, in case—
Although you are three light years away:

We found these fragments, an old oak box,
it's a strange one, no matter how often emptied

something always at the bottom
no matter how ill-treated, no scuff marks mar

this plain smooth lid: opened to this letter
see the writing, almost disappeared:

Your hand crushing mine, our lips never kissed.

PARTIAL TRANSCRIPT: THE REHABILITATED SCIENTISTS

We've not seen again the likes of them here.
We renounce facts and now wander with myth.

We swiped, before the blast, you better, too
        those signs pockmarked into walls;

we renounce replication or numbers.
We only try our best to help the sick.

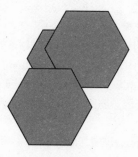

PHOTOGRAPHS OF PRISONERS

We walked knees bloody
masks torn; coats thrown
down to the bare stone ground—

no chance of ever going back,
none at all: ≈≈ / ⌂⌂.
our scribes wrote: ≈≈ / ⌂⌂.
≈≈ / ⌂⌂, be it resolved ≈≈ / ⌂⌂.

We did not ask for mercy
that Grand Hall, we heard them:
≈≈ / ⌂⌂. Their sayings,
night after night, and—above:

Cold-Heart-Wolf Moon,
laughing ≈≈ / ⌂⌂.
calling us, our damned visions,
close, closer: ≈≈ / ⌂⌂.

See you inside, this we sang out as—

COURT RECORDS OF THE LOST

Our skulls cracked on that granite
blood flowing—if at night, a traveller:
we knew him as the Lord of the Taverns,
girls flocked to him; women fell—

In his hands a book of magic, black bound:
El-Khemi, and geologic Time—
      all the great sagas, copied to disc, thrown down:
  the Western Ghats, rivers, far vistas—

Epics written in blood-ink, then singed wisps—

No escape or running free:
his gaze, his hand strong enough to crush men.

Gods watched from a stone bench, seated, rolling
dice, their laughter, thunder—
  how they longed to see such peals:

Era, epoch, eons later, and only that one time—

Although we had been gone for years
eyes shining, our rough hands cupped a seedling

ankles shackled, we bent to kiss our earth.
That stretch of coastline, laser-cut and fading——

BILL OF LADING FOR MASKS

Eastbound train jammed full of unmasked people
glances, those indeterminate voices—

Faster, faster, the snow-covered ground rose
higher than any tower, North Wind stinging

Her shawl undone, arms clutching a newborn.
We watched in silence as she tossed him up

already stilled, pale small fingers frozen
chilblains on his small toes, we had to burn

right there in the centre of everyone
oil-can rust, coal grate, orange flames flickering——

And then we went our separate ways, the night
steps resolving into steps, further from——

No one to see our broken smiles, falling
We'd remember—the power of the sun.

SCRATCHED DISC: RECORDING OF THE CAPTIVES

The men said to each other,
    "When your house is on fire,
        you got to scream—"

The women hunched in trenches, ready to
  shoot, fighters incarcerated, they said

  no use to reboot that power station.
  Those supply chains disrupted, all our food.

  Together they called, for years evermore,
  it were the Battle of Kingsway, it were——

THE NOTES OF THE BEEKEEPER'S DAUGHTER

They burnt all our hives; they killed my mother
With her last breath, she made me write these down

She taught us edge-magic, twilight and dusk
dawn or the hours just before, tilted
entry points, lines, horizon opening:
We'd race to the West, to time the sunset
We'd kneel, eastward, even when overcast
She told us to spin, turn, counted centres
the gap between thumb and index, sextant
in silence or in song, we stepped forward
daughters of the light, our breath, vibrations
that carrier landing amid gunfire
kneeling and blindfolded, against a wall
        three women, three men, their heads bowed, hands tied
She told us: fingertips to throat, temples
Circular, soft gaze at the moment of—

Oracle, beeswax built, tended by bees
Palace, those golden corners, six-sided
common and circular fit: tensile cell
those combs hanging wild, hunted, split open
heavy with nectar and pollen, straight lines
on the surface of—round, waggle, tipped scent
flower to flower, thy sweetness, a trail
irregular, murmuring to the sun
o new queen, o dowager drone, take flight
your cocoon spun, sealed royally and milked,
        swarmed, a drone to mate, hatched each thousand egg:
time, then, the turning of this earth, ripped sting
ox born, honey fed, forever to sing.

THE MAP OF THE LAST KNIGHT

Midnight, a train station, and outside
candles in a shop window, shadows
torrents of rain, cobblestones, lone gunman
sunrise, cathedral and a crow calls three
letters written, tiny, script, red ink, smeared pages
that Tower bathhouse, crescent moon and waxing
dripping to red, sealed parchment, trembling hands.
Believer, they were told those secret names.
Resisters, run. Run faster, they all cried.
His knife, sharp, light, edge to fold, pulled tight and
gasps cut off at the quick, footsteps, cold stone:
weavers and their spells, waterfalls dancing
cavern underground, from where we would return.

VIDEO REMNANT OF THE MIGRANTS

We set sail, star-guided, messages sent
below deck, nimble fingers curled paper

pushed spirals, long-necked apertures, green glass
once we were a part of the known world and yet,

our skies a torment, we could not see her.
Cyclones, the ravages of fault lines, cracked,

open——and we fell in——

The Parchment Scroll

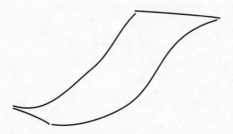

Glued together, parchment pieces as one
stained scroll, unrolled long, rough tattered edges
vellum frontispiece attached, faint inscriptions:

UNFURLED

Limitless circumference, we made this world
made this book and this book called you to us.
Six tapers lit, while outside, east winds howled.
Stroke by stroke, brush dipped into henna warmed—
Who will part our hair—soft, silken, to meet bone.
Bright morning sun: by evening, snow falls fast—
Faster, the years spooling ever backwards
with soft steps we will walk again, garden bound.
Banjaxed, shunned, cast out, we've burned our bridges
crossed, over, into——fled Perimeter.
We've longed for refuge: to sit, talk, drink—smoke
drifted, spiralling past our cold fingers.
Each flight from Mars, awakening, then
to find this oak box, these letters of men.

CHASED TO THE GATE OF THE SPRING PORTAL, 2050

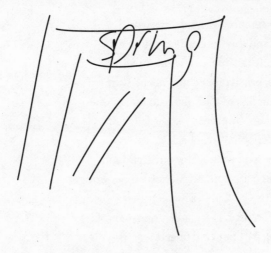

Roaming deserted streets, girls sang letters
Spin, rotate, tilting and orbital, Our Sun—

Come ye, Aunty Pandy, sweep and cough
Come ye, Aunty Pandy, sidestep, and masked.

Oh, for skies on lockdown, air fresh, leaves green.
Homeward bound we promise, our hands still clean.

Girls and boys, soon to become beggars, call,

IED *baby, your bombs, our arms, boom!*
IED *baby, inside, outside, boom!*

THE GREAT ABANDONMENT

It were a coming together of drought.
It were a virus let loose, lock and key,
    those protein receptors, encoded and—

It were fissures in the earth, deep fault lines.
It were mass migrations, lost belongings
    that child set down, the waves of a beach.

It were any number of armed militias,
roaming as temperatures soared, then the ice.
    Those roaring forest fires, farms let go.

We kept telling ourselves, unprecedented.
Over our shoulders, long looks at the past.
    Those Beggar Boys with their songs and their paint.

Aunty Maria, her seeds, and her bees.
She searched for scientists, we watched them bleed.

Jumped the fence

THE FIVE CATASTROPHES

By water, the soul
Tsunami, seepage
Cascading, eroded

By fire, the eyes
Scorched, singed
Blasted, burned
To melt—

By earth, the body
Trembling, split
Collapsed, on knees
Tumbled and crushed.

By wind, the voice
Blown, sifting syllables
Winnowed circumference
Made square by four

    Ripped, torn, worn, howl—
    It were the Battle of Kingsway, and after———

FOLLOWERS OF AUNTY MARIA

We who would walk Perimeter, those crows
a chorus, under feathers fluffed. Outside,

Rentalsman, honey locust, bare stands,
the thinnest trunks, Consortium-approved,
   roots shallow
      so as to not disturb—in our pockets
remnants, true felted, small quilt squares for masks,
Aunty Maria of Tyne and Church, all the streets now gone.

Fissured earth, snow a poison, yellowed edges, the shanty dogs
who would run to tear, what she held and rubbed
sewn circles, piece by piece—oh patch and mend—

Outside Perimeter no matter when
not enough tear gas to stop the screaming,
a group of street children found an oak box.
Someone told someone else: let's ransom this.

And did they find a way to cart that box?
One gang to haul, another to throw stones.
Guards at Detention Centre C, laughing.
Hardly a glance.

AUNTY MARIA'S CLANDESTINE HARVEST

In those days, she carried always,
The Book—at her hip,
My Garman,
she called it, banned.

All the Beggar Boys called out, *Aunty M!*
All those Sword Girls smiled and said,
>   *Come fight us for favour, come lose your limbs.*
>   No guards of the gate ever dared laugh.
>   In this way, distractions, to allow for:

cherished, when gathering Ninebark,
in star-shaped hairs, imported leaves
Physocarpus spirea,
city opening along one seam,
hardhack—small, glabrous, beaked,
she'd tramp under shrubs,
black hawthorn, doubly serrate,
mid-rib above deep green

she kept tucked close to her chest,
letters from the good doctor:
>   *Only the apical ends*
>   *... galea unfolded to reveal*

AUNTY MARIA TOLD US

Search for the Dove Tree, follow pocket-ghosts
—*Davidia involucrata*, three children chanted,
three replied, pick and pick—
at night, encounter, the last with such stories!

Once upon a time, long ago, Grand-Mère
travelled far-away-Eastern: tiny shops,
hidden shelves, a book, a trader, first
to describe. Oh, Night of the Story,
tell us more, tell us cordate and acuminate.

Help us journey, save us from the toothed margins,
    no balms for bitten.
Glabrous on top, Grand-Mère said of the story-tree,
    downy below.
Male, duo-male to female,
big bracts, the base, one long as the other.
Creamy white? We asked, together sang,
ovate pendulous.

Aunty Maria said, *Never count on flowers.*
We searched a monument with names.

This is what was told, handed down, petal to petal:
large drupes, woody crested seed, red bloom.

Aunty Maria told us to save seeds—
She told us to search for the scientists.

SCIENTISTS ON THE RUN

Now, at that time and in that place
we, sent to observe, wrote down
    their songs, those roving brigades
    Women of the Cleaning Class:

Required to Recite, as directed from Consortium:

We can see, in the pulsing places
Traces of his mordant graces
Where his tanks grind and crush
Scornfully, placate the dust—

We hid our data in abandoned shacks.
First, we measured for bees, then they died out.
Then we collected rain, droplets burning skin.
No snow on the mountains, bridges torn down.

The shelter sat where the wind bit sharp
    a crook-joint of land outside rows of—

There huddled a heifer, her calf
    ruffled brown hide   .
pressed close, a young goat, a fawn
    three hybrid gazelles.

We'd not last long, past fire, the things lost
    like this.

IN THE DRY, WE FIND OUR MOMENTS TO REST

Afternoons, side by side, counting Carder
Anthidium on white clover, borage, bellflowers
outside Rentalsman, tennis courts blackened—
to be spectator: luxury. A book, opened,
laptop and free access:

Sun of disquiet. Position calculated. Bombini's dance.
Where it once stood, gate opened, *Bombus mixtus*
Blackberry, buttercup, fireweed,
hairy cat's ear, thistle

Of demonstrations, nothing. The populace, un-
willing, no more, the people, dis-
satisfied, uneasy, intent on survival, a dis-
parity, only in the coveted sectors behind
barricades. A ground offensive.

OUR COMPARATIVE STUDY: THE BEAUTY BUSH

At noon the tennis courts, wet with rain, rare:
we counted eleven honey locust,
branches thickened with moss.

Six bird nests, omens—forget-me-not—
Long-tongued, the distance between
Short-tongued, not quite reaching the blooms
Kolkwitzia amabilis, signals of distress.

The glossa with terminal flabellum:
In long-tongued bees, the lorum is V-shaped and the mentum is
In short-tongued bees, the lorum is not—

      Alone in her condo out by the Good-Bye River,
a woman, chair-bound, reaches for cardamom,
        brown hand trembling—

Mornings we sit side by side, her kitchen table, Rentalsman home.
She asks us to read: the scattering scents of a Great Companion,
bruised Time   unheeding

OUR OBSERVATIONS MAY WELL GO UNHEEDED

Before the first Catastrophe, to keep track of—
yew bushes, simple varieties mass-planted

These trees could not know April's time of dread,
the cold, a keepsake, all such portents.

Parks regulated; Consortium yielded. Autumn. Long the dry—
at the community garden, only one hive, small masons'
colony-Heriades and struggled for months.

Each time of day telegraphed
messages, sent according to slant of light, rasp of wind:

If summer, direction turned, where each follicle would rise
            (and wind, with its name removed
If against winter, bend,
where a hood without fur,
            (many gathered to melt snow, before poison

Toss a little dust! No month end safe enough to ward off
behind the tennis courts, sheltering ditch, three Douglas firs.

In August, girls with sticks would beat out the nest
    abandoned. Not one person would swear to seeing
    the swarm.

BATTLE SONG OF THE STREETS

We that assemble: Consortium banned.
Cardo, stipes, galea, we whispered.
The City, our essence, cacophony,

pitched battles, informers and miscreants.
Our footsteps crushed wild thyme, boots cracked cement,
ropes to scale upwards those high walls.

We wanted to be counted yet deplored
repetition: stick to stick beatings, blood.
Children as young as ten years old coughed, screamed,

Freedom fighter, terrorist, who's right, wrong?
IED *baby, your bombs, our arms, boom!*
When they came for us, our bruised hands held

pass cards once coveted, once accepted
at the steps of public buildings where scores
of protest put down. Many generations.

Outside Perimeter walls, Beggar Boys,
Sword Girls, too, battling Guards of the Fifth Gate.
There came a time, when soldiers rode, guns cocked.

By then everyone yelling the same words:
IED *baby, your bombs, our arms, boom!*
IED *baby, inside, outside, room—*

And then those children crying, masks ripped, torn,
Freedom fighter, terrorist, who's right, wrong?
We just want enough to eat, been so long.

Night after night huddled at the Fifth Gate
we let winds breathe, *cardo, stipes, galea*

around condo cranes, we wandered, spray cans
in hand, our heads bent, eyes downcast.

No one left to believe we were once scientists.

AFTER CURFEW, TWO MASKED SCIENTISTS, ROAMING

Now these two were loved above all else.
And what form, what shape did their touching take?
We asked in at bars along bombed streets, searching:
we drank nectar at a tea shop along old Cordova Street, waiting
we counted months, Time's dance, each end date auguring
mouths could function as antennae, lips to teeth, to sac or tissue—
most bees and aphids, some birds, too, we wrote.
We revelled in words, signposts, to inquire, simple as Hallmark greetings.
Down Robson we strolled, oblivious to newscasts, incoming pervasive
Outside where once the old library, Mega Virgin CDs and DVDs,
a busker strummed his blue guitar, and two women, hand in hand.
We ran the length of the park named after a football player become elected.
Waiting for curfew, we slid into sleep, under a sun that would harm us.
Proximal end of—and neglected in the literature.

Once too often after hours, picked up.
Arrested by the INVESTIGATOR. Kept.

ON THE DESK OF THE INVESTIGATOR

At these times, the Sun's illumination,
warmer than previous—
We took these notes, measurements forbidden,
all instruments, loaned.

Banned from Assembly, we as researchers
moved to stairwells, backyards, basements—
Perimeter, demarcated decades:

hyssop, woodland sage, penstemon—bee nests
contraband, we gather, those forbidden names:
the Tribe, Bombini, genus Bombus, Cresson:
    appositus, bifarius, centralis
scrapped, crumpled, torn, tossed, found,

our travels to her streets, we recorded
Pacifica: those allowed those Outside—

in giant letters, Consortium's eternal message:

We can see, in the pulsing places
Traces of his mordant graces
Where his tanks grind and crush
Scornfully, placate the dust—

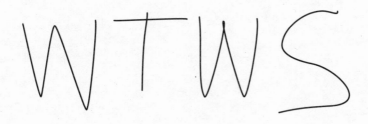

INSIDE DETENTION CENTRE C

The young woman sat rigid after her beating.
No salve soft enough.
And wore glasses.

Outside, Patrol assembled nightly, and regular.
Our young girls grown up under Rentalsman,
said Aunty Maria. We held our masks:
O moon, your sad steps

Again, the INVESTIGATOR:
we longed to feed him
      larkspur, large-leaved lupine,
wrap him blueweed, viper's bugloss—

In the lab, thumb edge to screen, began to decipher.
And swipe in, left, and again, swipe.
Rhythm defined an axis.
Everyone knew to keep their eyes downcast.

ORDERS FOR SURVEILLANCE

the necessary documentation.
Now an official, native to central
Informant for Rentalsman, events warning
heads bent, a cigarette, thumb to index
finger, not to point, to expound, listening:

murder, abduction, attributed to,
underground, away from,
Perimeter—

hours the rocks to warm, hours released
abandoned nests, where bees built their wax cups.
This plastic is to water
this framework is to subject
this agent is human, commodity
this repercussion, material
argument—glimpsed, only
           this object, to outside—
These representations, forbidden.
Two detainees. And their names
also effaced.

Outside Detention Centre C, those boys
hunted down for small crimes, they scream in hoarse voices:

IED *baby, your bombs, our arms, boom!*
IED *baby, inside, outside, boom!*

THE CURIOUSLY DISAPPEARING DOCUMENT

As found by the INVESTIGATOR inside this old oak box:
The more he touched the words, the faster they bled to fade
He'd put the parchment down
    even dropped it back into four dark corners
He'd pick the parchment up again
    each time his fingers met an edge——

From the medical records of——in the year of the reign:

Barrios, camps, Outside Perimeter: lineups, designated areas:
Tower Juniper, Tower Cedar, Tower Ambrosia
In Tower Ambrosia, a young girl, her name forgotten,
no one calls her, she is never spoken to—
Small build, dexterous, black hair, eyes slanted at their corners.
She never laughs, head bent most times, building things.
She calls them Finds. Her teeth, bones, unexamined.
Afternoons the heat: dust, that acrid curtain, wind whips red,
she finds places inside culverts where no streams
 fingers fast into hoarded, stolen, saved:
her six wheeled machine, scrapped aluminum,
prized at the site where once Safeway,
    The Battle of Kingsway, a song—
Fireside, she calls her toy.
There is no one around curious enough to ask—

Unnamed, without words, a series of lines, her pauses, dot-dash...
Long miles away, further down the coast, at Consortium Lab JPL
the designers study data, fascinated, curious and excited. All their codes.

TAKEN FROM THE NOTEBOOKS OF AUNTY MARIA, AFTER
   THE SCIENCE TRIALS

Not to be believed.
Those rumours.
My idle tales.
About the good doctor, nary a word.

Techniques for measuring abundance
although *Apis mellifera L.* and leafcutter bees
Megachile rotundata F., not native

Not a drop of honey, not a morsel of wax

—that very day the people of Kingsway began to rise—

Although not permitted: asters, yellow mustard
I have taken shrubby veronica, white clover
I am still able to transmit:
purple toadflax, sage and calendula

Perimeter assigns a schedule
when the rain falls—
leaves bear holes, burned.

—and at first light

they made us watch a thousand suns

collide———

OUR TESTIMONY ABOUT AUNTY MARIA

Yes, she was Outsider
Yes, she was kind to vulnerable others
Yes, she took risks, defied order, resisted
Yes, she yearned for something
Yes, she was willing. And sacrificed.
Yes, she, curious, made mistakes
Yes, she stood up, at what cost
  to herself.

Yes, when asked, we told the INVESTIGATOR
In the Before-Time she was a housewife.
He didn't believe us.

TO BE CONFISCATED: THREE HOLOGRAM PLATES

Plate #1

We Told
Ourselves
We Knew

This Day
Would Come:

Plate #2

After that first bomb, they tried to help us
Surveillance drones sent self-care packages
air quality and running water tests
proved inconclusive: we restarted though—
One day a mother ran out to the park
Look, she said. *I'm just tired of all this*:
little by little, we turned things back on
Ladies from the Patch 'n Mend Brigade laughed
Each you time you work your faucet, look twice
Keep your buckets handy, rainwater counts!
We learned to dig shelters, hoarded supplies
Those Patch 'n Mends mocked us; these chains will end
Consortium restored our wireless
at least our thumbs could scroll androids, and then—

Plate #3

A thousand cities, those streets, where houses—
and inside, closed circles, families, hands clasped
—and shake, soils into space, water pressure
on—and tight, tilt and slide, rupture, great waves

      —then the houses fell, and cities collapsed
      from deep inside Perimeter, we heard:
They filled our bee boxes—they slashed our hives—
we'll come back—in twenty-five-nine-two-oh
—and shake, soils into space, water pressure
on and tight, tilt and slide, rupture, great waves—
Come ye in, airborne, they whispered, lips bled,
after, masks and hoods, masks and hoods.

SONG OF THE SCIENTISTS

Side by side.
We never dreamt to walk with vagabonds.
And so, we took rooms in the city and—
We were reduced to very little
Months earlier, we drew the tarot (terror) card.
There was no going back
We had lost almost everything
Everything changed and happened at
Reasons were obscured by fancy
We told ourselves the worst realizations:
Dawn: most mornings brought pain
We knew we were surrounded.
The only field wherein we might—
Walking the length, a perimeter
Gesture as migration
The men called out to us and we ran away.
Later in the month, the moon
Vilified, we looked to the sky
Only to see a broad-faced blow-up doll
Full cheeks, thin lips, high heels
Control of property was beyond us
Often, we thought of that tree by the—
That woman cradled pine cones in her apron
Her mask hanging round her chin, blue cotton.
Train tracks varied in their hot metal grooves.
The ground gave, by way of fissures, deep cracks:
We imagined there had been a great tumult
withering bluestems, no sighs heard
And so, we roamed, the Collect, calling, *thuja, thuja*
Plantings done years ago——

AFTER THE BATTLE OF KINGSWAY, THE BEES

In the woods, a clearing—where we gathered
measured circumference, grove of cedar,
Douglas fir, redwoods, giant sequoia,
orange trees imported, illegal—
This were the time known as waiting.
From Rentalsman, we, survivors, and masked,
friends since the outbreak. Aunty Maria,
her spectacles cracked, plastic caressed,
kneeling, arms to hold linen, stitched over,
immersed she spoke of honey lore: meadow,
white boxes, pallets of—do this, she said
and take—blue hyssop, straw skep, sage.
Memory, a boxed wind chime, windowsill strings
pulled, lengthwise crescendo pine varnished rain.

POSTED ON CY-BOARD #6: AUNTY MARIA'S LAMENT

Stand and scroll these pages, what's left of us.
Be as we once were, flick, tap and swipe, quick!
If you are forced to remain, leave word here.

See to it, that these names are not erased:

After the first Catastrophe,
   long after the battle, the bees:
Enquiry! Diverse as water, and plastic.

O bring production, she was heard to sing later
save seeds, scavenge glass, jars to hold,
those who seek asylum among these giant trees—
The name sequoia, the name cedar, the name Douglas fir.

        And given,
            and given.

THE LAST KNOWN OBSERVATION REPORT

Outside, then, abundant end—
Inside, Beauty's roots parched
blooming—

Alors, fin abondante;
les racines de beauté desséchées, floraison

ثم نهاية
الجمال وفيرة كسرراب بقيعة يحسبه الظمان الشعبية، ويوجد
بالفندق.

    Let all evil die and the good endure

CAPTURED AT THE GATE OF THE SUMMER PORTAL, 2052

Chained, we sang, *Before is also a place*
Transport planes to buses, freight trains, shunting
railway tracks bombed, rebuilt with old iron
dry pine cones fell, unrelenting and sad.
Baghdad to Paris, east to west
reserve armies of labour, social unrest——
lone stragglers, a handful of Beggar Boys
one ragged little girl holding hands with
the good doctor, chalice grasped to her chest
covered with canvas sacking, bits of cloth
banned now from practice, she pledged to heal them,
the poorest families, sick with fever
those who stood at the back of the line shared
crusts of bread, telling tales of the Before.

Chained, we heard those Beggar Boys singing faint:

IED *baby, your bombs, our arms, boom!*
IED *baby, inside, outside, boom!*
Freedom fighter, terrorist, who's right, wrong?
We just want enough to eat, been so long.

(translated from the French.)

THE GREAT DISPERSAL

Transported Paris to Pacifica
captured and released, then captured again.
Aunty Maria and her glass jars, gone.
We found that doctor, hours before dawn.
Midnight across the river we heard them
Seed Savers with their song, heard far and wide:

Always, it were beginning and ending
That were journey, migration over months. The years—
That might be more than one lifetime
That season were a pattern, revealing
That many were, and twisted, and turned
That wine-dark river, that wild shoreline, tamed
That mountain range, blotted from view
That mother root, tree uprooted
That park bench, that concrete walkway
That endless game of chess. Queen to King
That floral arrangement, that left-behind object
That stillness in the bedroom
That earthquake disaster, that coming calamity, rivers and mountains
That deep ancient built-upon lake, lake without name, name known
      only by
That transmigration, that outcast slumber, that permanent exile, that
      bus-riding underclass
That liminal, white into black, brown into light into darkness:
      When everything happened—

THE GOOD DOCTOR, AS POSTED ON CY-BOARD #6

To Whom It May Concern

—although scorned and fearful of—
I found myself and sought them
    marauders, vagabonds, traders, riff-raff,
     brigands, invaders—survivors, they save
       seeds in glass jars.
And at the bridge of locks, cut off, waxed paper
    Still redolent of honey and the flowers—
     documents and escape, a series of borders

Once, would have been unthinkable, now we are close bound
     enough—
I've discovered Colony Collapse.
I've seen the despair of Queenless.
I've seen oceans overflowing, then sink,
smelt ice, the sound of it cracking, then—
I've hugged close, glass vials and my microscope.
I've told Beggar Boys and Girls: *This is a chalice.*
They laugh and point, they help me barter glass.

Signed,
Dr. A.E. Anderson.

THE GOOD DOCTOR IN PARIS

Sweltering heat, torrential rains, trees, stunted.
Inside the city walls, five clinics bombed.
Long after arrondissement destruction,
Perimeter a hazing ground,

Inside her battered clinic, what remains?
Only the good doctor and the parts to her chalice.

Those items found,
will be of that kingdom(e):
    broken hive, two aged empty chestnut conkers, hairy halves. One
        hardwood nut.
A seedling pine cone, needles
    still green. Empty husk, auburn gaping—
astonishing, to our doctor:
    when peering into reserves of contraband substance
the plastic of a freezer bag
    [brand name removed at the request of Consortium]
    heft of hive, destroyed, fragrant—strong smell,
    to be captured, from container HIVE F
there, at the exact time of looking
    out from hexagonal, dirty white and webbed,
black sac-body—faded label marked, *Mrs. Maria of Church at Tyne.*

Curfew alarms ignored, the bar open
at Café M, Dr. Anderson seen
    writing in her notebook
    pages folded to reveal a letter:

Dear Aunty Maria of Church at Tyne,

I am sending a boy to you, with seeds in a glass jar.
Kindly send word, when you can, of my chalice
last seen at——.

Attention! cry the street children, diesel
rags soaked, *Molotov!* Rocks, twigs, IED *baby!*
One slingshot—abandoned in the mud.

THE GOOD DOCTOR, WITNESS TO THE FATE OF CHILDREN

I refused to stop posting health records
premature babies, their third eye, bulging
Consortium banned all clinical trials
One by one the beggar children lined up
They thought cooperation meant hot meals
Trembling, blood-spattered, I wrote out their words
My eyes filled with tears, that was the moment
I told them later, they looked up and smiled
Shadow walker, my hair plaited with smoke
Ash biscuits on my tongue, dissolving grief:
left to die in the middle of the road.
This they repeated just under their breath
Who will come for us, the children asked me.
My gaze steady, I told them, only death.

Outside Sword Girls sighed, derisive, in chains:

IED, *baby,* IED.
Your bombs, our arms, boom!

RESISTER STATEMENTS PINNED TO CY-BOARD #6

Third attempt, connection intermittent

—a millionth of the cell's volume, spiked, cirque—
—we thought, *This won't happen to us*, and then—
—our bones irradiated light—sparse—cold
—almost transparent, we drifted across—
—Sector turnstiles, those NO-GO zones, we paused—
—at the Great Gate Called Destruction, we found—
—fluttering in the wind, scraps of paper—
—stray and stained, those ripped masks, sodden with rain—
—matchbooks gripped in swollen fingers, we lit—
—every affirmation, burnt to a crisp—
—we coughed, our lungs swollen, droplets of blood—
—*Sit back and enjoy the ride*, they told us—
—prisoners on those transport planes, Portal bound—
—we, the forgotten, all our stories, gone—

Hidden beneath Cy-Board #6

to you who will have arrived after
    if you read this, please leave word, or send signs
and then the bees hummed to us and we did

each note and entry, leading to the stars
banned from every Portal, we still escaped
that Wolf-Moon—laughing and coughing, droplets
Certain nights, the skies clear, a great many interceptions.

LOGBOOK OF THE GUARDS, PARIS FIFTH GATE

Signifier: 5 Rue Claude Bernard
coin Rue Pascal,

at the Café Mallarmé (formerly Café Léa)

Observed: lintel carving above the threshold
Will you deny day labour, light denied?

Observed: carved into stone under foot
Jumped the fence, you should too.

As confiscated: the notebooks of Dr. A.E. Anderson:

Should have proceeded so slowly
That the plants had not only
Cellular walls that could resist
This was immensity, the forests
Great arborescent. Those giants.
Evolutionary. Incomplete form.
Amid the cataclysms that changed us,
To the point of destroying our small homes.
As high and as constant as possible.
Ozone and carbon dioxide levels.
Outside sanctioned cordons, we were tested.
They will procure
our confession.

Everyone incessantly insistent,
about happiness.
Fulfillment in the mandated enclosures.
Today a group of children followed me.
I am resolved into a stoic attitude,
with a sure sense, the outer world:
Indifferent. Everywhere,
people are in chains.
They seem to really like it.

DR. A.E. ANDERSON, PERSON OF INTEREST

Of my grandmothers and my aunties:
Their voices calling me, memories' echo:

They sang lamentations:
Our seeds scattered to the wind,
our glass jars shattered.

For years they kept our plantings hidden.
As if it were a way station.
As if there were a sounding,
well outside the city.

Verdant,
a giant butterfly who spoke.

My aunties would make us walk to Kerr Street.
At dusk and at dawn we'd look to the trees.
Sequoia, their spindle kernels, shake, shake.

My aunties would say ever-after,
down in the town of towns:

If forced to use your knees,
assess all ground eventualities.

They were banned, and to no avail.

When Consortium takes over Portals
warned my aunties when I was growing up
No matter Paris or Pacifica,
they'd cough and laugh, then peer down and stare, hard,
everywhere, the old river danger.
After, they would just laugh and cough.
We never spoke of it, our masks, ripped, stained.

FROM A TRANSCRIPT GIVEN TO THE GUARDS OF
THE FIFTH GATE

I, Dr. A.E. Anderson, set down these notes,
in fear of impending.

Before Paris, I stood for hours in Verona.

—Said the Committee:
you will need to, and you must.

In that year I came to realize Science,
strength and threat.
Everybody reading everything, yet
very few with the patience to discern.

—Said the Committee: show us.

I have given over all my documents.
Betrayal, now my companion. Those two children!
Her small brown hand.
His gap-toothed smile, his beat-up runners,
       laces untied.

Never ask me again, the price of pain.

PARTIAL RECORD: THE WHEREABOUTS OF
DR. A.E. ANDERSON, TRACKED

Outside,
in the year of the reign 2052
in torrential rain, the winds, fierce
Dr. A.E. Anderson, face pressed against glass
Officine Grafiche de Arnoldo Mondadori Editore.
Dr. A.E. Anderson clutched letters sodden in her hands.
As if ink runs, scared of its dissolution—

Outside,
a Beggar Boy, his gap-toothed smile, sings:
A coin is corner enough.
Un coup de dés, ah-ayee, jamais, jamais
La Nuit, La Lune, La Terre
This is repeated many times.
Outside: some unidentified migrants.

Inside,
in the year of the reign 2052
carved over the lintel at the Bar of the Fifth Gate:
Un coup de dés, jamais, jamais

TRANSPORT PLANE MANIFEST

```
And his authority INVESTIGATIVE,
having first met those prisoners
thereafter known as XXXX.
```

Came the times,
and they were bad,
authority sent,
to search high and low
beggar children with their arms exposed
viral and connected,
transport planes commandeered,
resisters deported, penal colonies enhanced.

B-seen: Baghdad to Paris
them's in the compound
and that doctor, note-taking always.

Guards tracked her, long and hard, drone to device.
Her meetings with mothers of those children
this were written about.

To Pacifica then they came. Released.

PARIS TO PACIFICA, WE STITCHED OUR FRAGMENTS

cracked nails, bruised thumbs, black linen thread and bound
cracked nails, bruised thumbs, black linen thread and bound
cracked nails, bruised thumbs, black linen thread and bound
cracked nails, bruised thumbs, black linen thread and bound
cracked nails, bruised thumbs, black linen thread and bound
cracked nails, bruised thumbs, black linen thread and bound
cracked nails, bruised thumbs, black linen thread and bound
cracked nails, bruised thumbs, black linen thread and bound
cracked nails, bruised thumbs, black linen thread and bound
cracked nails, bruised thumbs, black linen thread and bound
cracked nails, bruised thumbs, black linen thread and bound
cracked nails, bruised thumbs, black linen thread and bound
cracked nails, bruised thumbs, black linen thread and bound
cracked nails, bruised thumbs, black linen thread and bound
cracked nails, bruised thumbs, black linen thread and bound
cracked nails, bruised thumbs, black linen thread and bound
cracked nails, bruised thumbs, black linen thread and bound
cracked nails, bruised thumbs, black linen thread and bound
cracked nails, bruised thumbs, black linen thread and bound
cracked nails, bruised thumbs, black linen thread and bound

DR. A.E. ANDERSON RETURNED TO PACIFICA

The first time I got away from—
Unstained, and not yet ochre,
Overcome by Incoming
Red became again carnal,
descended purple
Soon, I shall be punished.

The need for light brought me.
I am convinced others will, too.
Alone in the half afternoon, long walks
Toward the Good-Bye River, rising
No longer freshet—

FOUND INSIDE A CONSORTIUM LAB, PACIFICA

Partial Record #1

No perimeter walking allowed.
Not ever.
A long time since
what measure might come,
in the days ahead
partial fragments yielded
a small find,
once the park had been cleared
The hive. A honeybee.
Husked chestnut open
this, then, was treasure.
Only, if we could see—

Partial Record #2

Seen, decades earlier:
A group of them saving seeds and glass jars.

Partial Record #3

In the lab, before the Invasion, distracted
her focus is on substance, colloidal
against collusion, Aunty Maria prepares no explosives.

Outside Perimeter, Guards of the Fifth
They march lockstep, AK-47s, AR-15s.

They shout in hoarse voices, boots on the ground.
IED *baby, your bombs, our guns, boom!*
IED *baby, we'll search out your rooms.*

There will be no witnesses
save a set of designated trees.

LOGBOOK OF THE GUARDS, DETENTION CENTRE C, PACIFICA

Locator: Outside Perimeter, Pacifica.
As confiscated from the notebooks of Dr. A.E. Anderson

Gleditsia triacanthos
honey locust,
deciduous,
imported, smuggled in.

Locator: Inside Perimeter, Pacifica.
As confiscated from the notebooks of Dr. A.E. Anderson

Yellow sunburst honey green.
Cultivars thornless, less leaf, until late,
teleology as beauty:
pinnately compound, many narrow dreams, although
partially or doubly.

As Confiscated, four letters, attributed to a Mrs. Maria
    of Church Street.
These were burned and partial, smelling of smoke:

Singed Scraps:

deprived of water, in the cell, my tongue
found sixty-four large droplets, spilled. I read
names, by the light of a warden's candle:

Upright Douglas fir,
furrowed mature bark,
deep for scrolls,
I searched everywhere
a handful of brown cones,
grabbed enough for messages.
    A band of urchins.
    Highway's children,
      to take apart each conifer's gift,
      scale by scale
      to the seed.

STOLEN FROM DETENTION CENTRE C, PACIFICA

The smallest script within margins
To the city then we came, searching for—
Aunty Maria and Dr. Anderson.
Instead, we found these reports
folded inside a dossier, brought to us by
a straggling horde of beggar children
their hands bloody with scissor work.

First Report

Approach, said the INVESTIGATOR
A calamity borne in minute traces
Toward what disaster, amid plenty
No lack, a fullness
This capacity, surreptitious, a watching
Conventions dictated that she must
What is in a gaze? To be looked at
Edifice, means of transport, greenery
Seated, there were no tables or chairs
Seated, they missed the old oak pews
An Arborist of the Before-Time, a place
Sing(h), discern, separate, the peoples
All tender, the leaf, a stem, saved.
After, that is, before, there was arrival.
Disputed terror. Also, colour. Skinned,
History. Aware. Those men.
Turbans not mentioned.
River demarcating, what, exactly?
Perimeter, a statement of polis.
Always, the start of something.
Walked. Park, not graveyard.
The names. Saved for later.
Jaldi! Jaldi!

Second Report

Years earlier,
before each incident.
in the year of the reign
on the night in question
migrant workers,
an immigrant woman
her undertaking,
with care and attention
a handful of songs, only a few to survive.
We knew to look away.
Our eyes always downcast.

Perimeter is the not spoken. Aligned,
the lines become——
there is no mention of
the modes, whereby beggar children
their arms exposed, a number of clinical trials
transportation, a series
of numbers, there is no mention.

Third Report

Historic covert operations, banned
instead, drone surveillance instigated
satellite data livestreaming when on
everyone wanting access to printouts
no one with enough electricity
chronic shortage of lumber, dying trees
overwintering, a handful of bees
Consortium knew to ration supplies
stored infographics under lock and key
not one administrator prepared to
open up contracts and share any fees
those beggar children with their splice and paste
encryptions cut, saved, nothing left to waste
abandoned courthouses, cold marble steps
You bring the cash, they called. *We'll do the prep.*

RESISTERS BROUGHT IN FOR QUESTIONING

We admit to surveying, up by the Eve River

We all wore masks.

We hiked past
rip-rapped roads

stayed high up on trails,
logged to the water line,

covered in young hemlock,
red alder:
—that's how we found the river
—line by line.

Later inside Rentalsman,
    that Beggar Boy sent us word, inked
on saved scrap:

Consortium to order a thousand
    glass vials, import dollar-buddleia
young Douglas firs, tree farmed,

close to power lines,
radio towers visible,

western hemlocks also planted,
    coastal streams built over,
where coho once, pink once, chinook, chum, salmon, steelhead—

Once upon a time, we were together.

We admit we knew Aunty Maria

Outside, before train convoys—
Outside, crowded platforms.
Them with arms straight, hands empty.
Outside, waving is not permitted.
Gangs of youth wander, singing,
Un coup de dés, ah-ayee, ah-yee, jamais, jamais.

We glimpsed the edge of her cherry-red coat.

Inside, celebrations banned, yet
inside, she sat, her coat, Sears-purchased
many tokens saved.

Her skin taut brown
her cheekbones angled against
her scarf another red the red of
her youth, head covered, she'd pick bent across acres cranberry strawberry
blueberry and not harvested anymore.

Inside, she, our neighbour,
cropped hair grey-nappy-soft,
praise songs at risk
where outside the little bursts,
no one said the word, *gunfire,*
where marched a formation,
two militia, tanks down Vanness.

It were the Battle of Kingsway, we said.

IED baby, your bombs, our arms, boom!
IED baby, inside, outside, boom!
Freedom fighter, terrorist, who's right, wrong?
We just want enough to eat, been so long.

We admit to helping the Doctor

Enclosed within Perimeter, she'd send
us as instructed to Aunty Maria
the two of them found a way, back and forth
doctor to aunty gathering saved seeds,
the Long Hours, afternoon-time
    a holy mystery.

    Both of them to tell scavengers:
observation is ritual. Remember:

Butterfly's and Beauty's. Under duress
    these bushes will croon:
      Buddleia, Kolkwitzia amabilis—

Wing joints, we saw, azimuth circles and
Eights, antennae flattened wing latches rear
front claws, membrane, muscles, the thorax

    cuticle bands, tree's bole, dry crevice pressed.

We deny knowledge of her chalice

And came those workers and that woman to
dig a deep trench and fill it with these things:
component parts, old-fashioned and upright.
As directed in messages, seams ripped,
She told us it were her chalice, she said:
pieces for the eye and nose, lenses clipped.
Condensor and mirror, forward and sideways.
Rack stop, tube, glass vials, a set of slides.
She carried also, in her pockets these
scribbled notes:

On the night in question,
ten migrant workers, all male
were found to have—
An immigrant woman,
acting as citizen
her mother also—
Observations, surreptitious.
There was the walking.
A perimeter. A city park.

THE RESISTERS RELINQUISH DR. ANDERSON'S INSTRUCTIONS
FOR A CHALICE

Unable to withstand the terror of—
branding. See here, these plates buried earthbound
instructions retrieved, brush off this dirt, safe.

Here's a knife to cut, holographic dig
rectangle of sod, roots to hand, to dig
white worms squirm, and dig, dig—

these beggar children will help us, lift, dig,
back to the lab, electricity rationed.

What? Yes. No, like this. Wait. Like this.
Our hands will push the fire button, fast light
emitting memory, a set of pieces: chalice reconstructed!

From eye to tube, adjust, nose resting, look
down and into, glass slides, adjust, adjust—

To save ourselves from hot iron tongs we'll
do just about anything, it would seem.

AS NARRATED BY THE INVESTIGATOR

And so, in this way, I tracked them all down
    Portal Hoppers, trace devices secured
  everyone these days knowing
    the price of a hire.

    What use a set of spells against machines
     all the latest models
       Consortium-approved.

Take us to the chambers
Save us from the Guards

Take us to detention
Keep us from their tongs

None of us spoke.
In our hands, fragments, torn scraps of paper.
    Small vials of elderberry. We saved them
    to drink later, after our escape from Detention Centre C.
And hid among the alien corn, GMO and sprayed,
    at the far eastern wall of the Fifth Gate.
We'd brought with us the good doctor's chalice.
We'd whispered messages sent, just in time:
from Aunty Maria, rolled scrolls, glass jars.

Wash your hands, use your sleeve,
    sang a gang of Beggar Boys.
And we replied under our breath:
    Trust us now, you'll never have to grieve.
Out on the sunbaked tarmac, transport planes
    languished for want of fuel, where soldiers marched:
    Lave tes mains, utilise ta manche.
At dusk, no one left to hear Beggar Boys,
    IED, baby, IED!
    Who's right, who's wrong?
    We just want to eat
        —been so long

AS REPORTED TO THE INVESTIGATOR, DETENTION CENTRE C

Informant #1

Yes, there were three of them, lab assistants and
they worked to record, light waves on those plates.
Yes, we searched everywhere, beam splitter and
they stole from Consortium, two lasers.
Yes, she denied all knowledge: reference beams
telepresence, the last Ethernet, gone.

Informant #2

After many years, countless encounters
woman to woman, men also
she resolved to inoculate children,
in a futile attempt to share resources.
Variants of concern haunted each camp.
Each hurt a public wound, reprimanded
for crossing lines; she dared to share her skill.
She broke all the rules of the Healing Guild.
Outside Perimeter
people streamed across borders, and sent
in their own way, any number of messages.
How to get their children to her
by any means necessary—

Informant #3

Tucked behind the cover of her journal
sketches for a chalice diagram, pulled—
Well before the first catastrophe, she
began by studying all the Beggar Boys
usually in small groupings
always outnumbered in their language.
She found herself stuttering, unsure how
to replicate their rhythms, to fit in
against Consortium rules forbidding speech.
She wrote down resister prophecies, signs.
Her messages to Cy-Board #6, delayed.

THE GOOD DOCTOR, AS POSTED ON CY-BOARD #6

To Whom It May Concern

Third attempt, connection intermittent.

We crossed out of Perimeter, borders,
hedges, train tracks, a long line of fir trees
Long after the Battle of Kingsway, survivors.

My arrest impending or so they say.

Befriended, this small girl brings me androids.
At night she squats beside me, chanting words.

I can only decipher a few here:

> *Right as rain*
> > *good as new*
> *Jumped the fence*
> > *you should too.*

Her poor left arm branded:

DESIDERATA

Beggar Boys to chalk mark Perimeter,
trails, boundaries, even if not permitted would allow for—
Everyone in those days carried within the names of—
All of them to pace dimensions: cell, chamber, park,
    yard, compound, plaza, a field, vast, the forest—

Said the mothers at the well, *Please not yet*
Said the teacher, bombed-out classroom, *Simple*
Said the three washerwomen, *Jump that fence!*
Said the resisters, deep in hiding, *Find that little beggar girl even if—*

Said the INVESTIGATOR, *Gold is its own reward*
Said the Guard of the Fifth, him with his cold blue eyes,
    I know just the girl.
Said the Village Spy, *Regret's a luxury.*
Said Dr. Anderson after she was forbidden to practise medicine,
You see, the both of them, in on it. Don't blame Betty, she was in love.

A GUARD OF THE FIFTH LURES BETTY, DAUGHTER OF THE VILLAGE SPY

His smile, slant, those looks, and sat close to her
And she, knowing that gaze, those cold blue eyes
Cascading petals, leaves, autumn to spring

Lamp magnolia, star-shaped too, imagine
Possession, interlocked, a fit, two joined who must
She realized; this is how he got them—

And careened toward abandonment
If only she had not fallen under.
Always, those surveillance cameras, third eye

He said in that language, when last, they had sat—
Together. Imagine, she thought, afterward, the power, unearned

The thing that would come, turning who could tell
Thinking back, she realized, and could not believe

Gate, lock, door threshold, alleyway, street corner
Imagine, being, so entranced, she shook
to think of trouble, the way his smile came at her.

Inside the tavern where they met, carved words
over the lintel where the liquor sat:
On that day, a hundred years ago, the people.

THE WORK OF DR. ANDERSON AS RECOUNTED BY
THE VILLAGE SPY

Outside that place, they lined up for hours.
All those children, what she doing with them?
Well, I won't lie, them Guards did pay me some.

My little one come home talking *chalice*
I checked her arm though, and made her promise—
I overheard them mothers, best I could:

It be our children, now what she doing—
Got them all going on about soap so—
What? Look at these masks we're sewing, all ripped—

Anyways, I said to this Guard of the Fifth Gate
him with those cold blue eyes, I know his type
What? Never you mind about my eldest!

When he asked me to point out the doctor
I laughed and told him to watch the colour
The colour of what? he said, voice real hard.

Oh, I says to him, *strawberry-blonde locks.*
Thought of that later when they shorn her skull.

Said the Village Spy to the INVESTIGATOR after:

I warned Betty about those Guards of the Fifth.
You didn't have to get her in with them.

Course I did what you asked, didn't I, then?
Turned in that doctor to help out my girl.

BETTY, THE DAUGHTER OF THE VILLAGE SPY

We followed that doctor in cafés, plazas,
Those trips by ferry boat,
small vessels not yet banned, to Island meetings.

We got letters, paper stored, sewn inside
coats, hemlines unravelling messages:

We'll come back—in twenty-five-nine-two-oh
Draco in three thousand, Vega in twelve

We took away her chalice and she cried:
For God's sake, don't touch those glass slides, they'll break—

At night we brought her water, crusts of bread.

Chained, that Gate, closing—we knew those portals.
We wanted to get a fair price for her.

We went up to the INVESTIGATOR.
He really liked hurting people.

He told us to vacate at first light, even if acid:
He told us to sleep on stone, touch texture
He told us to scavenge for wood, and name each branch
He told us to speak quiet, not wanting to name the sixth material,
broken, restored, broken again, and found.

BETTY'S STATEMENT

In the box, Detention Centre C,
handwritten with curlicues on yellow lined paper.

OMG. *His face.*
OMG. *His jawline, chiselled.*
OMG. *His hands so large, broad shoulders*
    narrow waist.
OMG. *His height, well above the others—*
OMG. *The colour of his hair.*
OMG. *His slant eyes, the coldest blue.*
OMG. *His long brows, lashes.*
OMG. *All I did not see, then, and now—*
OMG. *The way I'll never be*
OMG. *No matter how hard I try*
OMG. *His face—*

Well, what more do you want from me, anyways?
        You got my son. I got you those documents.
I told them guards who brought me here,
        it were first time in that pub.
I tell you; I tell you, I did it for love.
        Fuck you for laughing.
I don't care what any of them say now.
        I love it that he was a Guard of the Fifth.
He sat with his back against the window
and did not flinch when—
Well, yes, I went up to him, just like you said I was to
Well, yes, him with his back to the window,
        OMG his hair, the angle of his jaw.
What? No. I didn't. Okay. Well. Maybe a little.
He didn't! Well later when I bent closer,
        breath against his neck, fingers on his shoulder,
        words warm and he did not draw away.

        Wasn't that what I was supposed to do?
        We got her to you, didn't we?
        No one said anything to me about any chalice.
        Anyways. He set it all up for us. Just like you said.

DOCUMENTS OBTAINED BY GUARDS OF THE FIFTH

The Anderson Family, Paternal Side

There is an understanding between the estate
of Dr. A.E. Anderson, confiscated and—
Her father's family hostile to the farm
Consortium Executive and proud.

The Anderson Family, Maternal Side

Her aunties never wishing to reveal
Said Aunty Agatha to the women
gathered outside Detention Centre C:
Her mother was my niece and told me true
Here, take my baby, never ask me whose—

PARTIAL RECORD: THE WHEREABOUTS OF DR. A.E. ANDERSON

Outside,
where once leaves would fall
in the year of the reign 2055
beggar children shuttle
city to city
a kind of English.

From their small hands a clutch of messages.
Smiling they barter, they dash in and out.

Outside,
hot sun baking hills
in the year of the reign 2055
in drought, wind scouring a coast
helicopters overhead, rotors search:

Dr. A.E. Anderson, bent at the waist, in a dry gully
strawberry-blonde hair blowing, grit laden,
hands shaking, she pushes back strands to see
the INVESTIGATOR, striding toward——
eyes shaded, his mask, black, stitched with red thread.

DR. ANDERSON, RENDERED TO THE INVESTIGATOR

Locator: Pacifica, in the year of the reign 2055

On the Desk of the INVESTIGATOR:

Authorization: Guards of the Fifth Gate
Number of Survivors: undetermined
Successful Rendering: 1
Q-Camp monitors: active
Name: Dr. A.E. Anderson

Dossier:

Video testimony: Betty, daughter of the Village Spy:

Anything, I said. For him, I'd do any—

Found by Guards of the Fifth Gate in an abandoned farmhouse:

One black leather notebook: cream-coloured paper, spidery handwriting:

Sixth dose extraction successful and I—

One scrawled note, inside seam, black wool coat:

Those Soap Makers Knew

This, outside the City gate:

$RHRF$

DR. ANDERSON REFUSES TO ANSWER

This set down, this:
I never intended disobedience,
avoided state television,
still Incoming came on in,
pressed itself and made known,
      unavoidable.

At the end of a regime, in the year of the reign
      in between spaces, forward, back,
about to, almost gone, not yet begun
in the shadow of, barely discerned
incomplete, faint, emanations
messages from rocks, stars, birds, trees
discarded tarot card stepped on, too fast a gait
      not slow enough.

Borders, gates, security, entrance, visa.
Denial, locks, interrogation room.
Guns, inspection, the necessary passes.
Waiting, in line to stand, and stand again.
A set of questions, incomplete answers.
Exhaustion, not able to explain why.
In the fact of hostility, unknowing
those assumptions of, and conspiracy.
A glance, guards pointing, their masks, N-95.
Perimeter built, once was to ensure.
Then broken, reconstituted, walled off.

To be outpost—to be outsider, hated:
    to be occupier—to be dominant, to rule:
    to be unwanted and afraid.
To be present at the end of an era, epoch,
    to continue into calamity, into twilight, heyday long gone
to line up past splendour, eyes downcast,
        to become ghost, traces of—

DR. A.E. ANDERSON, AT DETENTION CENTRE C

As Video Recorded:

Dear—

      This letter written inside this letter
      last night I gazed at the photo you took—
      on a tablecloth, red and white, fabric
      outside the frame, a border of domestic.
      Sweet kitchen tableaux: newspaper edge, folded,
      my name revealed, face imprinted
      brings pleasure, even though you told me
      straight enough, you'd rather your own!
      To bite the hand that feeds. I excel:
      these terrifying imperfections.
      They call me and at my age and—
      No worries. I've ripped out the notes where—
      and in time, will remove more.
      What they want are names.
      And I refuse.
      Daughter of a Consortium Executive.
      They hate that.

FROM A TRANSCRIPT ASSEMBLED BY THE GUARDS OF
DETENTION CENTRE C

I, Dr. A.E. Anderson
daughter of the Farm,
born in the year 2020,
brought up by Women of the Wishing Well

neither confirm nor deny
mention of the child
known only as a beggar girl.
Her small hands held by another boy, indigent.
Well, there are so many street urchins now.
Inoculation efforts suspended.
No reasons offered by Consortium.

I did not want them
to see me writing,

the number of unused doses obtained
the number of beggar children obtained
the number of hidden vials obtained

In fact, infected. They lived in Tower Juniper.
Although banned outright,
several women pleased with me
passed their words without books,
lips to mouth, eyes downcast.
And spoke of rain, burning.

Forbidden medicine, I have taken
this habit of climate observation.

THE INTERROGATION OF DR. A.E. ANDERSON

INVESTIGATOR: WHO ARE YOU WORKING WITH?

Yes, it is true and I'm not sure how it happened.
So deep and three months in, based on nothing

INVESTIGATOR: WHAT BRAND OF SERUM?

Really, and you, on the other hand, always ahead
Science is a series of questions, unanswered.

INVESTIGATOR: WE WILL CONDUCT THE NECESSARY
   AMPUTATIONS.

Time, a perception, and changing—
I mean, the distance, between,

INVESTIGATOR: MAKE A NOTE TO PAY THAT GUARD
EXTRA.

and what I really want to know is—
You will see, these codes for what they are. Until

INVESTIGATOR: AND GET ME THAT WOMAN, BETTY.
USEFUL.

Perimeter, walked, and dug, the earth.
Every star a sun, she said.

DR. ANDERSON AFTER HER FIRST BEATING

The Tale of the Silver Sandals

I will bury all my childhood memories at the Farm, where once I ran
      happy and free——or, rainy days, inside the aunties' house:

    a pair of heeled silver sandals,
mesh straps
It were behind the overstuffed chair, chintz-covered cabbage roses
In the stillness of afternoon

He'd come up with us from Perimeter, my red-headed boy,
We'd lie down behind the chair
and——

My flowered dress, his white fingers on my thigh
silver sandals kicked off——
They were far too big for my small feet.

The Tale of Barnston Island, as Then Was Called

Journey is a time for observation,
Aunty Agatha would intone.

She'd try and get us to wear our masks.
Then we'd all start giggling.

Pluck, Pluck, sang her nieces and nephews.
A great congregation in the kitchen.

Buttery roast, the butchering early:
platters of plenty: carrots, chivvied greens,

crisp, sweet, salty, succulent memories just
beyond reach, the more held, slipping over

that oak-beamed doorstep—threshold to the past:
inside abundance, outside, east winds blew—

troops conscripted from children: they coughed, too
tired to rise up, no one ever knew.

DR. ANDERSON AFTER HER SECOND BEATING

All My Aunties

All my eggs in one basket
and my hen is named Mathilda.

It were Aunty Agatha's farm,
where we all lived.

In the Before, with her other nieces and nephews.
And before Aunty Pandy, mind you—

Aunty Agatha's recipe book.
Lined foolscap pasted into a black book:

    Icing sugar melted
        into bread

Recipe borrowed from a friend of a friend of Aunty Agatha.
    Name unknown,
      brown hands trembling, her children's children taken,
        into their bodies, injections
        Consortium-approved,
        all the long ago.

Those West Coast Trails

We hiked those trails, carrying our equipment.
Young women followed us, writing down notes.

Youth, yes, an itemization:
Sunglasses, gear, stance, voice, stories, blisters, long-limbed and smooth.
Yes, golden on the ferry to—and from—

On the threshold the east wind brought rain only twice
In many weeks, four months, count

Young women hiked kilometres per day
Eager to tell me, they gathered round

We were in a rhythm, they: young and glowing
Me with my strawberry-blonde hair, flowing—

Freshwater lakes they said
You should do it, they said, the stars.

Castaway Beggar Boys and Girls sang soft,

magical island of primrose and mist
bribe the Ferryman to give you his list.

Dr. Anderson Hallucinates

Said Aunty Agatha, *You will fashion for yourself a new name.*

I laughed then, never dreaming I'd be forced to—

She told me to crane my head toward the moon.

And so, it came, the terrible time
without ceremony

Little did I know, all my training, all my instruments
taken, bartered, sold.

Consortium told me I was no one to assume a title.
Consortium forbade me to heal the sick.

DR. A.E. ANDERSON, BROKEN BY A BRAND

As Decreed by Consortium
   —Order signed by the INVESTIGATOR,

to gouge, iron tongs used by Guards of the Fifth
Gate:

As procured, a statement by Dr. A.E. Anderson:

Singed skin, branded, the smell of my own flesh.

They needed beggar children, all their names.
Consortium decreed, those who would receive
Variant resistant, prototypes grown.
It were purely a business transaction,
or so they told me. And I disobeyed.

DR. ANDERSON LEARNS OF THE KEPT WOMEN

Different hexes, jinxes, bad-luck scorning
Forget black cats and ladders, she said: run—
Torn clovers, that golden knot uncut, spilled salt
Melted Bucephalus, coins of the realm
Mirrors, satchels, that freckled peddler's ring
Cow's bells rung past midnight, rowan berries
Clay figurines, blood spatters, pinpricked tips
Clipped, braided locks; six red eyelashes, singed
At that moment in the Capitol: guns.
Behind the back aisle of the grocery store
Seated, he looked upwards to that painting
Horseshoes inverted, clattering cobble—
Factory girls wept saying, *No matter what,*
each of them survivors of his abuse.

DR. ANDERSON, AS KEPT BY THE INVESTIGATOR

Partial Video Surveillance:

Dear,

You were always steps ahead.
Your words echo, their timbre
a location. You stood close to me, that time

we were in the gallery, in the park, inside a crowd
your urgent breathless voice
in my ear, *Oh,* you said my name
you told me you were with a man
such excitement in your vibration
and I scoffed
did not pay attention—
see, you are my age so will know what to do.
Do you ever fret about, say, the neck?
Or under the eye, or lower down: hips, the backs of thighs, belly?
Or do you strut in confidence?
Sustenance is the gaze. You taught me that.
Years ago, you said, *I need to have—*
and without, I'm not
and again, I just dismissed you.
Oh, I understand now. That gaze, those moments
before touch, there is a kind of energy—

You will never see these pages.
I keep them here, in Rentalsman.

Online, I search for and cannot help
Panic, he won't keep me here much longer and then—

Villagers say I am beating the odds.
I'm obsessed with surface
It is a territory.

Some days in the city, outside,
every woman is better than, is the one who will
for whom I'll be, or am.
I refuse to count the number of times he looks at me.
Days when we return from the Commons, I allow myself to forget,
prisoner.

DR. ANDERSON, COLLABORATOR

Only the length of shadows to tell time
his voice softest when he is about to—

A small scar on the inside of his thumb
Guards shift their weight, metal clanging on stone

They cough, dry dust swirling under locked doors
sliding open to this room, the sound of our breath

Strawberry blonde, he says, his hands on my hair—
With swollen fingers, he traces congealed
the first letter of my name, whispered,
Call this your tattoo, his breath warm on my neck
of the brand he placed on my back, he says,
Just like the other girls.
Save, I am not.

As for me and my shame, I have no such
——distance from the fact that I told him.
Names and locations and yet,
what my body accepted my spirit

did not. Find me here in Rentalsman though
a kept woman.

DR. ANDERSON SINGS HERSELF TO SLEEP

How many miles to
How many roads to
How many years since

Oh, at night I've viewed the Inner-Net.
Search, click, names of names.
I will create my Obscura
        Content and repeat
Page view, deeper, the number higher
Each search, something, someone, from the past—
        Your face, your words, the things you made
        Your life and its place
Oh, at night I've searched, name by name
Others you've known, I track them down
        Action is mortification.

Lurker, and timid, last night a photograph.
You, standing with others. I found their names.
Could not hold in memory. Pencilled in
Clicked and clicked—

Today, your power haunts me
Assessment endless, an itemization of parts
Ratio of, contrast to
My flaws
And I know I will return
Drawn to image, defeated by image—
This place of no mercy.

DR. ANDERSON: TESTIMONY

Afternoon, month ending to blend
I read these notes left in an old oak box:

*Un coup de dés
Jamais, jamais*
Outside a brigade

chained, they dig trenches, singing.
I have seen them at the close of day
chance, hazard

lodged into the body's softest
most secret places
Imagine, said the women held with me.

Imagine, I said, recanting
and knew a different set of rules. Approved and applied:
my lab bombed, my chalice dismantled, pieces—

My name is Abigail Ellen Anderson,
grandniece of my Aunty Agatha.
My parents perished in the year I was born.

Yes, it's true.
Aunty Agatha once met her, that girl locksmith.
She said her name was Bramah.

THE LAST DREAM OF DR. A.E. ANDERSON

that girl stood; feet encased
    newspapers torn

abandoned, the lab where once
        traced—

they would wake, dreams hollow
    filled with other things

un/birthed, un/sought, nevertheless
    longed for—
his beauty frightened me, she said.

And I'd forgotten: my own first name, stitched
inside lower left shoulder seam, I.D.

tagged, Dr. A.E. Anderson, mask torn:
Come away, Abigail Ellen, says Aunty Agatha:

—*Courage, girl*, for the way forward—

THE LAST WORDS OF DR. A.E. ANDERSON

and I was warned
afterward, the aftertime—
   I entered that tunnel, those echoing footsteps—

   tank turrets swivel left to right, take aim
   Molotov! scream one-armed boys, their small bones
   on the mountains, fire—in the Courtyard, dust.

Catastrophe is an earthquake of the soul
   how the body stores pain, vein to arteries,
in the streets, masked youth,

   those children of university professors
Pacifica to Santiago, all along our coast
all my warnings, after, ignored:

   distance a space between two lovers.
They told me I'd succumb and indeed, I gave over—
bereft I said and said again: your lips will still sting from—

The prosecutor will state I gave succour to an invader,
the defence will claim I had no choice, standing
   and alone, my stained ripped mask hanging off one ear—

They predicted I would be stripped of privileges:
In the basement of the hospital laundry, one care worker—
   after, they tortured her, too.

My resistance will amount to little,
only a name bestowed upon:
Abigail—sweet little beggar girl-child
she'll be mine.

THE SPY'S TALE TO THE INVESTIGATOR

By this time so used were we to wattle and clay,
we always knew to begin that way

We longed for plastic, the bend and bright
of foil, and aluminum strong.

Oh, the sheen of nylon, its many uses,
us with our shopping bags and containers.

Multifarious! No one saw steel. Iron maybe.
Wood hoarded. Lock and Key.

Yes, we heard a name, Bramah.
No, not once was seen.
Just an old aunty with a Pippin File.
Guards repeated what she said:

I've come for my girl's girl
I'll open your lock with a click and a twirl.

THE INFORMATION

On the Desk of the INVESTIGATOR:

Authorization: Guards of the Fifth Gate
As produced: One Beggar Boy, age un/known
Successful rendering: 1
Tower Juniper: Monitors disabled
Name: Un/known

Resists all attempts at translation, the INVESTIGATOR writes in
    his notebook.
Outside the compound, a group of Beggar Boys chant.
Jamais, Jamais

Report as Delivered:
diverted medical supplies, resorted to Consortium.
stockpile inventory proceeding.
all transport routes secured.
six cases of serum located.
names of subjects, as inoculated, forthcoming.

To begin, a meeting of the shareholders.
A trillion orders of, and successful.
All the doctor's clinical trials ended.

Air transports arranged, their private shuttles.
The necessary transactions signed, sent.
Catered wine, a sumptuous lunch: pre-takeoff.

Embossed in gold on their indictment folders,
This is what we have built, and it is good.
The name, Anderson, A.E., then removed.

Outside the Tribunal, chain gangs digging
trenches to prop up Consortium's wall.
In shackles the captured resisters sing,
This is what we must build, forgive our work.

Outside, Beggar Boys chant, IED, *baby.*
Inside, the Tribunal's Secretary declines to call
　　　　any witnesses.

AFTER THE MEETING, A VERDICT

Sword Girls, cheeks tear-stained, chased by Guards, screamed loud:

Let all evil die and the good endure!

Inside their pockets, fragments of torn text
a letter, untouched by Guards, too unsure
to search those quicksilver limbs, fast moving.

Outside the Detention Centre, armed men.
By nightfall a ragtag bunch of Beggar Boys
haul cans of stolen red paint:

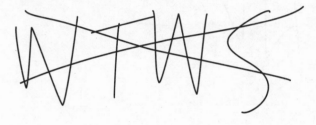

AFTER THE VERDICT, ORDERS: SIGNED & SEALED

On the desk of the INVESTIGATOR:
a set of gold rings, engraved, pressed red wax:

Ransomed Healed Restored Forgiven.

Swirling red capes of the Guards
embroidered, *Charity, our rifle shots, not fired*
yet—

R H R F

THE EXECUTION OF DR. A.E. ANDERSON, 2057

The Song of the Stonebreakers' Yard

That rapid gunfire, close to her chest—
blindfolded and slender, the way she fell
they'll burn her notes, they'll kill all who tell.
They called her the brightest, they called her the best.
Bring them the dullards, no stories to mull
her strawberry-blonde hair, shorn to the skull—

SMUGGLED OUT OF DETENTION CENTRE C

Dear Aunty Agatha,

After the Battle of Kingsway—
    how I wish—
    and to have told you, everything
    and cannot.
I do not know why on certain days—
Time, the hours, distance, the miles—

To recall moments in this unending—
I dread knowledge, act of discovery
inevitable————not yet
ever-present————not yet
oh these my silent pleas
————world without mercy

I found this little girl, beggar Outside Perimeter.
If I should die before—
    oh Aunty—
        take her away from this place.

Signed, with affection, your loving niece,
A.

REPORT OF THE GUARDS OF THE FIFTH, AFTER A SEARCH
FOR THE LITTLE BEGGAR GIRL

We knew to search them huts, wattle and clay,
we always knew to begin that way

We longed for concrete, squared strong, clean corners
Outside Perimeter's edge, only camps.

Oh, the sheen of nylon, its many uses,
zip-ties handy, swift stun guns held hip height—

Multifarious! No one saw steel. Iron maybe.
Wood hoarded. Lock and Key.

Yes, we heard a name, Bramah.
No, not once was seen.
Just an old aunty with a Pippin File.
Look, she mumbled into her shawl and said:

I've come for my girl's girl
I'll open your lock with a click and a twirl.

We all laughed. Didn't mind her words, not then.

FOUR AUNTIES AT PERIMETER'S EDGE

—rain landing, courtside abandoned, gates swung
—asphalt cracks extending—we found her bag

—*the good doctor*, we said, and bent to reach—
—*fissure, this*, we whispered—outside Tower Juniper

—we held the brown hand of that little girl
—we told those children as was taught, and said:

Just Call Her Abigail

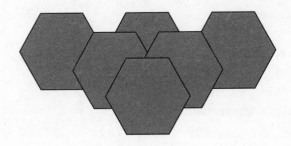

AFTERMATH: RESISTERS AND MIGRANTS IMPRISONED

As found in a witness statement, struck from the
record by order of the INVESTIGATOR

—from the doctor formerly known as A.E. Anderson

~~Don't let them forget how to make soap~~

Don't let them forget how to make soap

~~Don't let them—~~

AT THE END OF THE PARCHMENT SCROLL

And did they then weep, sat back on their heels
fingers rubbing those rough tattered edges.

And did Bramah say under her soft breath,
We'll find Aunty Agatha and ask her—

And did Bramah say, *Sweep everything else
save this parchment scroll, tied up with red string—*

And did they ferry that old oak box, empty
under night's cover, no moons to shine bright—

Well, some say it different, they say:

Bramah with trembling hand folded the scroll
her warm skin, the Beggar Boy's hands, so cold,
they smoothed parchment, tied up with red string pulled
from Bramah's pocket. The oak chest hauled out,
lighter than expected. Under night's cover
they fled the farmhouse, looking back only
once where howled a lone wolf high in the hills.

>>>>>>

138

The Adventures of Bramah and the Beggar Boy Continued

RETURN TO THE WINTER PORTAL

Seasons of mists, those Beggar Boys sang soft,
magical island of primrose and mist
bribe the Ferryman to give you his list.

Thatched eves, winnowing wind, high in the loft.
Shift-Tilt: our seasons ran cold, marble halls
We called out, chained, from departing buses—
Draco in three thousand, Vega in twelve

Those Beggar Boys replied, their small hands raised—
Draco in three thousand, Vega in twelve
Marble halls, where seasons ran cold, tilt-shift

This present, that is our future
We'll come back—in twenty-five-nine-two-oh
We'll come back—in twenty-five-nine-two-oh

BRAMAH TEACHES THE BEGGAR BOY ABOUT THE STARS

From Draco to Vega, one degree of—
    arcs, those rising places, seventy years

plus two, on the horizon and to the right—

    clockwise, wobbling like a dying top, if

lips were to call out, no one would hear such—
    messages, extended circles, one journey

to conquer the years, thousands and thousands
    Equinox: we were called to travel and——

HONEY HUNTING IN THE WILDS OF THE WESTERN BOREALIS

Where the forest floor fell, a huge red oak
combs refilled nearer to the tree of bees
circling into figure eights, eastward line.

She told us of a forest: ash, poplar, beech, birch
knot holes, up high in hemlock, wild pouring—
men, she told us, stole thousands of pounds.

She told us of mutant variants, genes wild
by then no one to measure or observe
space missions private, Consortium reserved.

They filled our bee boxes—they slashed our hives—
when we come back——Draco in three thousand

    Vega in twelve——

SEARCH FOR THE BITTER GREEN WILLOW

That shade a distant star, parsecs away
around the earth, and to the far first moon
a journey to the Sun in eight minutes

What measures shall we bring, what instruments
parsec counters, they sat her in a room
she who found Neptune: four hours, roaming—

diurnal and divided, the Night said:
east to west, rotational, great sphere turning
above us no fixed points, only the light—

In this way we learned to outmanoeuvre
armies, battleships, Consortium tanks.
It were the woman of the willows, she

taught us how to navigate by the stars.

>>>>>>

BRAMAH AND THE RESISTERS

She left the Beggar Boy with Grandmother.
She grew in fame and stature with her tools.

Locksmith extraordinaire, her hands steady
her pick and twirl, her golden Pippin File.

She helped them to survive, siphoning off
funds from her Consortium contracts given

over to Grandmother who warned in visions:
impending raids, inspections from the Guards.

Many a time she was called before the
INVESTIGATOR, she never faltered.

The trouble with you, he said one cold night.
—*No one as fast enough, no one as skilled.*

Although questioned about that old oak box
her face impassive, her brown eyes downcast.

THE BATTLE OF THE WHISPERING TREES AND AFTER

Everyone sidestepping everyone else
that long steep fall, down-down-down
where no birds sang, or only the one:
everyone keening the same old song
full-throated, ice-hacked, that lake sly as sin
entrapped, they'd say later, diaphanous:
locked doors, footsteps echoing, a hand raised
voices recorded on tape; suitcase lost—
Banquet table regulars, we sat full
those several trips, an array of choices
special occasion parlance, gleaming knives
our eyes held: her shining skin, her bright hair
We made sure she never, we made sure—
Bramah, we said, *take us with you*, and she
did.

We took turns carrying the book of stories.
We carted, pulled, pushed, preserved, that oak box.
From the lips of the Beggar Boy, no words.

And did Bramah return to us. She did.
And Grandmother shared her Threshold Magic:
each year a code, a gate, a lock and key:
all pushed us onward further from Perimeter
honey locust, oak, flowering dogwood
anonymous, soon and after, imposed
little gods, usually spiteful, who watched
tacit unseen when we gathered round to—
learn from, and listen to, once upon a
time: brief encounters, close calls, near misses
we hid seeds, we bartered for glass, we dodged
those Guards of the Fifth Gate sent to track us.
Always on the run, we fled to the hills.
Drones and satellites no match for our spells.

WHAT BRAMAH LEARNED, SHE TAUGHT

He stood, swarm surrounded, then fell knee-first
acacia hidden, we emerged, straight
to his body, touching each welt, red ridged.
A thousand stings, salve circles, fingered skin
to receive the wounded or to comfort
strewn across the veldt, hundreds of men
through thinnest of cloth: arms, necks, backs, stung
at night, she made us write out our word lists
paper scraps, pencil stubs, boots smeared with blood
Bramah crouched, console set to the stars' light
she tapped code to call the ship back to us
crushed thyme underfoot a scent we carried.
Did each of those men have names, she would ask—
to bury the dead, to sing of this task—

Our killings done with mercy.

GRANDMOTHER HEARS NEWS OF THE FOUR AUNTIES

And in that time long after the Five Troubles
And in that time of torrential rains, windswept
And in that time of colony collapse
    extreme climate variability
summer droughts, the land parched, wells gone septic
She heard the aunties still grew wheat somewhere
    far Outside Perimeter, by ferry
        how to send word to them back there, before—

She overheard a Guard of the Fifth Gate,
    Some crazy old woman, her Beggar Boys
        we moved them on because of their chanting:

When the North Wind blows, Agatha
    remember, remember
      gold and silver scissors, honey in small pots
When the southern breezes sigh, Tabitha
    silk ribbons, running red
banyan and oak, linden and ash
Magda from the east, Maria from the west
    copper thimbles filled with mead
sequoia seeds shaken, salal leaves pressed

Meet Them at the Wishing Well
What They've Seen They Never Tell.

All this Grandmother memorized, although
she took her time, before telling Bramah.
First, Grandmother wanted to tell her own tales——

AROUND THE CAMPFIRE CALLED *IF ONLY…*

We gathered to hear:
Bramah's grandmother, who laughed, coughing:

> The Tale of the Knife: A Disappearing Trick
> The Tale of the Ice Box
> The Tale of the Little Golden Spoon—

When we said, *Tell us*. She just laughed and coughed.

And did we lean in closer? We did. We did.
Grandmother just coughed and laughed; her mask torn.

Nah, Nah, some tales are mine for keeps, until—

And did that Beggar Boy lean in, eyes round as saucers?
He did. And Grandmother just coughed and laughed,

Now, now, you take Ravi, my voodoo doll
Hide her from Consortium: rip her seams.

Inside, ivory and gold, parchment scraps.
These her foreshadowings, never say they're dreams:

The Tale of the Girl and the Disappearing Streams

Her distances vast, her steps measured long
south of the Equator, never rising
unseen star, yet she knew to turn herself
what once was North, directly overhead.

Mind's eye dilated, this she had been taught
to wait—before her feet met tundra, poplars
sun-dappled green, a few stands of red oak
long lines of alder, their sticky sap sought—

in her quiver, a thousand arrows, each
Calisto, Arcos, forearm to shoulder
semicircles and faint, ending in pairs
the scent of water, stones marked pungent, sweet

east wind, north south, her eyes, instruments
evenings in springtime, as then were called: she'd
hunt for the first bright loganberries, lips
stained red, mouth open, her tongue water fed.

The Tale of the Girl with a Thousand Pockets

Once upon a time,
   there lived a girl
      who owned a coat with a thousand pockets.

This girl was tall, her hips narrow as a Stripling Boy,
those ones who gathered acorns at Perimeter's edge.

At night under the cold light of the two moons,
the Chief of the Acorn Boys
met with the Girl with a Thousand Pockets.

Rumour was that Acorn Boy was the bastard of Betty, the Village Spy.
Everyone knew that Betty was always fooling with one guard
   or another, always hanging out at that Mean Old Fifth Gate.

Anyways, there was Acorn Boy,
also known as Bloody-Eyed Jim.
There was the Girl with a Thousand Pockets.

Each pocket held a key or a lock,
or a locket and many other such things.

Before a Portal Opening, saying the words,
   First, full, last—
under the unwinking gaze of two cold moons,

Acorn Boy and Pocket Girl
escaped the Guards of the Fifth Gate.

So much underhanded trading going on!
Seeds for keys. Glass for lockets,
pennies for pliers.

Many a cold two-moon night, they gathered, boys, girls,
and few of them who said, *We're in between.* ·

In a circle they sat, leather satchels
opened to show Pippin Files, tweezers
picks and drill.

One after the other, boy, girl and in-betweens
told stories within stories of Bramah
she of the Gold and the Green.

Oh, they said, *her long black braid*
her quick hands.

One night, one year later, those two moons hid their light for hours.

Bloody-Eyed Jim crouched low amid tall grasses.
These grasses, planted by Pocket Girl's great-grandma,
were known as the Disappearing Weeds.

If you crouched low enough, you could go invisible.

First, you had to kiss the ground and pull out one weedy grass clump.

Bloody-Eyed Jim was about to grasp grass and heave up,
when suddenly, in blew a gust of North Wind.

Clouds flew across the faces of those two cold moons.
It were the Time of the Great Barter.

And there amid the Disappearing Weeds,
stood the Girl with a Thousand Pockets,

her rainbow-coloured hair streaming down
either side of her narrow shoulders, down to her narrow hips.

Watch out, Jim! the girl cried.
Then she fell face down into the weeds.

Bloody-Eyed Jim ran to the girl.

His leather-toed boots touched her silent limbs.
The girl lay face down in mud.

In between her shoulder blades, a lone long knife.
With one strong tug, Bloody-Eyed Jim pulled,
warm flesh, cold steel.

Bloody-Eyed Jim turned the girl over.
He bent to her face, lifted a strand of hair—
oh, those soft shell-shaped lips:

Bloody-Eyed Jim heard three soft words: *First, full, last.*

Then the Girl with a Thousand Pockets breathed her last breath.

He grabbed at her coat.
He pulled her pockets;
he pulled her coat down and off.

Bloody-Eyed Jim leapt up—
then he paused, and bent to the dead girl,
he tucked his hands into her pockets.
He pulled out two gold coins and put the coins on the girl's eyes.

"May you sleep the sleep of Ever-Forgetting,
    rising one day, unharmed," Jim said.

When Bloody-Eyed Jim looked up to the far edge of Perimeter, he saw
three tanks and one hundred horses, sent in by the INVESTIGATOR.

Men and women shouted and pointed.

Jim flung the coat of the Girl with a Thousand Pockets over his own shoulders.

He ran away into the wind, far across Perimeter's edge.
Never a Guard could catch him, as long as he knew the *first, full last.*

When the North Wind blows a song,
up to those two cold moons, shadows leap.

Some say in the shape of a tall willowy girl—
there she is, look up, dancing with the wind.

The Tale of the Girl with Far-Seeing Eyes

This is a story recorded one day
by that blind girl who saw everything and

by Bloody-Eyed Jim: his hands all over

things stolen, bartered and traded: androids,
cracked laser plates, them WiFi access codes

given over to a Guard, then stolen back by the trader,
Jai-Ishmael, great-grandson, cousin, twice removed of, oh well never mind.

Alas, when Aunty Pandy came, she took
Jai-Ishmael and with him this story.

All we got from him then was hacking coughs.
We sat with him but at a distance,

you understand.

Him on his big belly, no one to turn him over.

The Tale of the Boy with the Red Canoe

Grandmother said, *Now pay attention to this story.*
The trader Jai-Ishmael stole this story from another trader.
That trader: such a big troublemaker. Grandmother coughed and laughed,
   He fell out way past the Winter Portal.

The Boy at the Lake stood to greet us, his face unsmiling.
Why have you come here? he said, his eyes brown, his black brows straight.
In his hands he held upright his red canoe.

When we squatted at his feet, tired from our journey—
the Boy at the Lake said,

I am the Boy of this Lake.
This is my Red Canoe.
My stories are not your stories. You have no right to them.

We looked up at him then, and began to get ready to leave.
The Boy at the Lake nodded and said, *Not this time. Not this place.*

Even though we forgot to thank him,
in the end, he gave us his Red Canoe.
We never saw him again.

The Tale of the Girl Who Slept with Spiders

Cobwebs criss-crossed her purple-brown lips,
strands grey-white, sticky lifted, her trembling

hands to morning shadows, dew outside, signs
ankh, amulet, revenant, her words held,

rubbed, stored, cast away, ashes on the wind——
What star is that who burns so bright above?

This the Beggar Boys chanted, *lock and key.*
In the courtyard of Perimeter, found:

one leather satchel, the finest calfskin
pockets for a set of locksmith tools, gone.

Let all evil die and the good endure

And Bramah said, *Grandmother, this is my favourite of all your stories.*
And Grandmother just laughed and coughed.
And the Beggar Boy said nothing at all.

THE THINGS THEY DISCOVER ABOUT THE OLD OAK BOX

No kick or thump to dint that wood frame.
No matter how many openings done,
on nights of the full two moons,

if opened by Bramah or the Beggar Boy
any number of finds to tumble out:
one ruby ring, bartered for glass and salt.

One gold spoon, sent to a Guard of the Fifth,
during the time of the Excise Inspection
he never bothered much with them, then

and Grandma laughed, stroking the plain box lid
  You best mind your Ps and Qs around this—

INSIDE THE OLD OAK BOX, THE BEGGAR BOY FINDS
ANOTHER MAP

His fingers touched each word, thumb edge rubbing
parchment, a red wax seal, insignia.

His index finger might find messages—
He kept his eyes on the markings, black script.

His hands held a torch, unwavering.
And Bramah read out loud:

geometric and geological
Giza or Romania
mass distributed, thin shells floating
geoid with a sphere
projected to the closest point
those last land surfaces
survival a calculation
digital mainframe degrees
40 52 North
34 34 East

We will sing of Mercator and no more.
We will urge you to find the exact centre of the earth.

And from there, look up, and from there the Seasons,
all our calculations, memory, an arrow

hurtling toward a set of distances——

INSIDE THE OLD OAK BOX, THE BEGGAR BOY FINDS
   A DOCUMENT

From the Medical Records of——in the year 2050

Barrios, camps, Outside Perimeter:
lineups, designated areas:
Tower Juniper, Tower Cedar, Tower Ambrosia.

Inside, a young girl,
   her name forgotten,
no one calls her, she is never spoken to—

Small build, dexterous, black hair,
   eyes slanted at their corners.
She never laughs, head bent most times—

She builds things. She calls them Finds. Her teeth, bones, unexamined.

Afternoons the heat: dust, that acrid curtain,
      wind whips red, she finds places inside culverts where no streams,
fingers fast into hoarded, stolen, saved:

her six-wheeled machine, scrapped aluminum,
   prized at the site, where once Safeway,
         The Battle of Kingsway, a song—

Fireside, she calls her toy, no one around curious enough to ask—
Unnamed, without words, her fingers tap, pause, dot . dash –

Long miles away, further down the coast,
   at Consortium Lab KTS: the designers study data,
         fascinated, curious and excited. All their codes.

THE OLD OAK BOX, GONE!

Wait, said Bramah, *I must rest for otherwise I might faint*

And eeriness comes over me, she said
Her black braid glistening in the candlelight

Crouched beneath the crooked lip of that cave
The Beggar Boy ran his fingers over words

The slant of them! Each stroke and lift and sphere.
His eyes never leaving the face of Bramah:

her tears brushed aside and then the oak box—
locked, carried, hidden, stolen, found again.

That morning when we awoke, all things changed:
the oak box gone; the tattered scroll of stories,

disappeared.

The two of them wide-eyed, hearts pounding fast.
Drones overhead, lights flashing and a voice

Consortium commandeering return
Quick, cried Bramah, *stay close to me and run—*

HIDING OUT WITH THE NIGHT STITCHER

Seamstress of dreams, butterfly-catcher, tied
string, pieces of felt, pounded, shaped into
memories, made whole: tie that bit, wrists, ankles
Translate your discoveries, she'd call as
her east wind sang through dry cracked houses where
room after room, empty, save mirrors: they'd
run only to, and never, not once—
she told them they'd better avoid the house
where in a circle sat the oldest crones—
gender-indeterminate, lipstick smeared
some chemical compound from the Before:
Time an equation: they knew to travel
years to find that oak door, gold-embossed crest
Run, cried Bramah, arrows stinging her chest.

BRAMAH TELLS THE BEGGAR BOY SHE MUST LEAVE

Oak, and throw down: split acorns
The Beggar Boy runs to catch and hold.

Catalpa, pendulous green overhangs
The Beggar Boy trips and falls. Gets up again.

Cedar, scent remembering-forgetting, sent—
The Beggar Boy, panting, rubs his ankle.

Elderberry, a cordial, goblets of fire—
Bramah's aim is true. Down the guards and up they go.

Linden, that long avenue, shaded.
On horseback and in tanks, unrelenting.

Laurel, that time of the heroes return.
Bramah binds and carries and finds the spot.

Bramah wipes away blood from her shoulder.
Oak and cedar. The Beggar Boy fights back tears.

Bramah tells the boy: *Find your name, son.*
Midnight, years later, eons forward, you'll

run tundra, you will fall to your knees, still.
Get up! Run to the Gate of the Winter Portal.

Find the boys who sing,
Until the rains arrive, and we survive
Until—

BRAMAH REMEMBERS A LULLABY

Ice-fed, wet yarns felted, a loom of stars:
In the hour before sunrise, three ribbons
They will come to you, as I am singing:
Winged tapestry—tied strings, salvaged pieces—
Divining wheel, a thousand threads entwined.
Your name golden brown, you will snap, pin, tie
hidden: cascara girl: camas, birch, pine.
Woman, seated at a bench, soft cloth pulled—
Woman on a platform waiting, eastbound
time to touch, that absence fastened, cast-off
    before every door, every key thrown, every gate locked,
forward, backward, a thousand needles cleaned
your hands in the Before-Time, thread to loom:
your eyes sparkling, our names cut and held.

BRAMAH'S SECRET

What is your name? With me always.

તમારું નામ શું છે?

Tamāruṁ nāma śuṁ chē?

What is this? This knowing lodged beneath my heart

આ શું છે

Ā śuṁ chē ?   Another journey to the past

Who will stitch my seams,

કોણ મારી સીમ ટાંકો કરશે?

Kōṇa mārī sīma ṭāṅkō karaśē?   To find my story

Bind my wounds,

મારા ઘાવને કોણ બાંધશે?

Mārā ghāvanē kōṇa bāndhaśē?   I am leaving, I am leaving

coda   Goodbye, little Beggar Boy—

My heart aches

મારા હૃદયમાં દુખાવો થાય છે

Mārā hṛdayamāṁ dukhāvō thāya chē

(mara boh dukh che)

>>>>>>

MANY MILES TO CROSS

And this loneliness: we whispered the song
and this anger, held. We engraved letters—

And this shame, we wove a cloak, white feathers
invisible to the Outside World, yet

barbed points dug, stuck sharp, meeting skin, our hands.

When Bramah turned away from the Portal,
she saw for the last time, that Beggar Boy.

All these years, she called to him, receding,
I've never learned your name! He smiled at her.

He turned into that dark alleyway, waved—
Then ran to catch up to Grandmother and

somewhere along that long passage, boys sang,
Right as rain, good as new,

jumped the fence, you should too—
 Un coup de dés, jamais, jamais——

THE INVESTIGATOR

Today I found a diary, black leather.
Inside, cream-coloured pages: and this note—
    My dear Aunty, take this beggar girl.

Yesterday's arrest: a yield of two boys.
The one with the gap-toothed smile has proven—
          uncooperative.
             In any case, I shall find that satchel,
                  those tools will be traced and that old oak box.

Can it be on nights of no moon, restless
the INVESTIGATOR tosses and turns
never one to admit fear he'll not say
words heard on the cusp of a southeast wind:

Whosoever finds us, with a kind heart.
Whosoever drops us, they'll always part.

Bring us a cloth to varnish, bring us jade
All your gold and rubies, in us, never fade.

We'll bring you a story, and then disappear.
Lift us, don't drag us, you'll never know fear.

AT THE CHAPEL OF THE STONE AUNTIES

Masked boys, arms branded, the air dangerous,
dropped, no one to dare breathe, not ever our spells
could save our girl, her name whispered, snow deep

drifts knee high, against the wind we trudged.
We added the names of dead scientists.
Brigades of children marched tower to wall.

Not even our old magic to protect
shawls worn threadbare, we wrapped ourselves up tight.
Have you ever seen our stone faces bleed?

Freedom fighter, terrorist, who's right, wrong?
We just want enough to eat, been so long.

Not any one of our years over one hundred
        could rise and help them, in their time of need.

THE LAST SONG AT THE END OF THE KNOWN WORLD

Once upon a time, there lived a young girl.
Her hair glossy black, her skin honey brown.

Lost, those faraway hills.
That blue ocean. Snow-capped peaks.

Diving, the girl touched depths, then up, up to sunlight.
And fast, she ran away—all around her,

faint echoes ringing, those Beggar Boys singing,

Right as rain, good as new,

Jumped the fence, you should too—
 Jumped the fence, you should too—

AT PERIMETER'S EDGE

Evening drops down blue-black
 two moons rise bright and clear
 only a ragtag bunch of beggar children
  huddled against Consortium's Wall:

Before Guards move them along
  before the drones blare out curfew orders
before the night patrol scan, in armoured tanks:

There's our Bramah, gone with the sea.
She's tumbled Portals, looking for her tree.

There's our doctor, she's good and dead.
Wrapped up her chalice, knocked off her head.

Hey Aunty Agatha, where's your little girl?
Hey Grandma find us; we'll swirl you a secret

that little Beggar Boy's not who you think
to market, to market, Consortium stinks.

Hey Aunty Agatha, weave us our fates—
Hey Aunty Agatha, threshold to gate—

PART TWO

>>>>>>

>>>>>>

>>>>>>

Abigail Discovered

RUIN, A MAP FOR PERIMETER

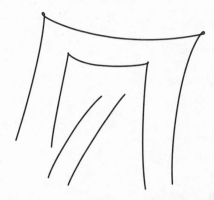

Long lines shuffling past bombed buildings, ice shards
    piercing the skin against a fierce north wind.
Inside, the Guards of the Fifth Gate roll dice.
    Outside, children dart between drifts of snow.

Freedom fighter, terrorist, who's right, wrong?
We just want enough to eat, been so long.

On a hill rising, Perimeter wolves.
Midnight, that second moon shining silver
Winter Portal, blasted open—
Upright Douglas fir, furrowed mature bark
split open with fungi, gigantic spores.
Covert, we scrape samples, only no one
left to test or measure; we search anyway
brown cones, deformed tips; our hands hold hidden
each, a message, we share on pain of death
On the highway, on the run, we gather
we take apart each conifer's gift
scale by scale, to the seed, 2057—

AFTER CURFEW, THOSE STREET SWEEPERS SING

After Aunty Pandy swept us all up
Consortium Minders stood in a row:

hand to hand: one ice cube, dropped left and right,
paper to paper, dry towel to wet—

melt! The heat from our hands leaving our skin:
they taught us hydrogen on the outside,

shivering, our breath in puffs, they taught us
bond to bond breaking, trapped crystals in space.

Sugar and salt, our bellies stayed empty.
Sugar and salt, our cracked lips licked sharp rocks.

These schoolyards in snowdrifts, these doors all locked:
Come, Bramah, with your golden pick and key.

Come, Bramah, with your Pippin File, your drill.
Crack open doorways, save us from all ill.

THE FOUR AUNTIES OF THE WISHING WELL

—said Aunty Agatha:
First frost, stay apart, you'll live to see the—
withered grasses, falling leaves, use your sleeve.
My scissors, sharp; six honey pot smears.

—said Aunty Tabitha:
Cotton scraps, nylon bits, pull your fraying quilts.
First frost, stay apart, you'll live to see the—
summer breezes, soft as silk, red dawn, running.

—said Aunty Magda:
river water dwelling, wood ash in lime
copper thimbles carried, beech twigs in brine
withered grasses, falling leaves, use your sleeve.

—said Aunty Maria:
my seed jars all stolen, my masons, gone
Find me sand and find me pressed salal leaves.
First frost, stay apart, you'll live to see the—

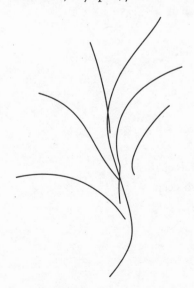

AS HEARD ON THE ALBION FERRY

There's our Aunty Agatha never gets old
There's our Little Abigail brown and gold

Where's the good doctor, where is her chalice?
Consortium killed her, so much malice

Bramah's gone and left us, nary a trace
Oh Little Abigail, who will you chase?

There's our Aunt Agatha huddled in red
There's a north wind blowing, over the dead

There's the old Ferryman, sing him a tune
He'll not charge you coin; he'll call up the Moon

There's our Aunt Agatha digging a trench
She'll bury that hammer under a bench

The river freezes, she's warm underneath
Tidal her messages, cast on the beach

There's our Aunt Agatha huddled in red
A handful of nieces, so it is said

A is for Abigail found at the door
B is for Bramah who loves her the more——

Blow you North Wind, your ice crystals cut deep
Bide with our Aunty, she'll sing you to sleep.

FOUND PINNED TO A FAR WALL, PERIMETER'S EDGE

They watched us eat, small bites, the food to last
our confinement measured in months, then years.

To ban vegetables, except as grown by
Consortium: stamped and wrapped, GMO.

To note percentage change, temperature.
A clandestine activity. Science refused.

To begin in gardens, those TFWS——
Those Beggar Boys, sidestepping mechanics.

To water with amounts found, the rains, then
to marvel: succulents, gloss of outer skin.

Months later, forbidden to notice, so
we invented charts, refrains for the mind.

Outside Perimeter, those Beggar Boys
singing Toxic Breeze! Don't you dare breathe, don't——

FOUND: ONE OAK BOX. LOCKED.

Said the INVESTIGATOR:

Guards, get me that locksmith, bring me her tools.

Said the Guards:

She's nowhere to be found.

Said the INVESTIGATOR:

Blow it up, then.

They tried every explosive.
Nothing worked.
That old oak box sat without a singe.
Only one hinge bent, enough to pry open:

Here is what they found inside:

Stained Parchment, Engraved

These preserved words———as recited at noon:

Our inheritance: our family farm, landed
    the years a generation———before the Great Culling
    our chickens in their cages penned,
    a thousand tubers tilled.

    Our workers masked,
    still got ill.

All through the night incendiary bombs falling
    our windows shattered; our phone lines cut.

Outside, our children ran amok, seeking
quick, shelter, shattered timber beams falling
acres of dust, straw thrown up and falling
we heard their chants turned rough, turned crying, *Help!*
Mocked by young boys, armed by Guards of the Fifth:

IED *baby, your bombs, our arms, boom!*
IED *baby, inside, outside, boom!*

Cotton Scrap, Embroidered

Trouble is Fear,
double-edged ware

Fear is our fists
dare you to stare

Look at our fists
our blood on these stones

Trouble is Fear
we're locked inside here:

Hey Bramah, throw us your file
golden and green
bring us your key

Trouble is Fear
we'll get out of here—

A Blood-Stained Letter & Other Things

Dear Travellers,

Found:

1 journal——
only these ripped pages remain.
1 mask, left behind, decontaminated.
charcoal streaked and dusty——

These instructions, these three hologram plates.
Our supply of lasers long since depleted.

Fare Forward, Voyagers: Hologram #1

We transmit this encampment bombarded
last night's walk through minefields
light interferences, separate sources
transmission encampment no one recalls
enough morse code to make it worth trying

light interference, separate sources
silver under moonlight, slow-motion dials
many wrong turns. Inner harbour, bombed out
hotel refuge, blue carpet descent, down
a thousand stairs, cordoned, infection controls

security, nonchalant their devices
IED *baby*, beggar children chanting
wash your hands, jump the fence, don't you dare cough
alley barricades, waterfront unknown
sector name unknown, a child stares past us
light interferences, separate sources
we bend to him and then——sharp explosions

clutching at our cloth masks, we run toward
light interferences, separate sources
Perimeter's Edge>>>>>>>>>>>>>>>>>>>>>>>

Fare Forward, Voyagers: Hologram #2

Past midnight a dog barks lonesome, memories
flood all the zones—we huddle alone
night illuminated only by fire
place, a series of shards, we imagined
comfort, tea in fine china, all gone, songs

of the Beggar Boys, *un coup de dés*
jamais, jamais, they sing into the night
that time we escaped, it were a Poacher
his dog barking, at first, we paid no mind
only by the fire to realize late
the dog a hound, and the hound belonging
to Guards of the Fifth Gate, their faces shielded
—we pressed into the wind, again running
streets, mud rutted, torn masks, ripped blue gloves
glass, condoms, cast-off plastic flowers
a beggar child limped following behind
he was barefoot, shoelace tied lopsided
round his neck a copper key, he led us
to side streets, we night-walked into their camps
Spanish, Vietnamese, Arabic, French,
the children ran away screaming, *Wash your hands*
   ha ha ha, wash your hands—
   night illuminated only by fire
   we sang with them,
   IED *baby, un coup de dés>>>>>>>>>>>>>>>>>>*

Fare Forward, Voyagers: Hologram #3

—tires stacked, flame sparking rusted barrels
hands burnt, memory an inside ruse, fleeting
to finger cloth, squares cut, crumpled piles, worn
women squatted to touch, turning this way
Mask Makers' hidden camps, forbidden to—
as if making unleavened, bread-cloth, shared

A few contemporaneous notes
something about the need to save a chalice
diagrams shoved into our hands, trembling
streams of people, abandoning their homes
shoulder to shoulder, we followed their gaze
turned toward smouldering city towers

That's over now, that's all gone they kept saying
and kept moving, marching ever westward—

HEARD OUTSIDE TOWER JUNIPER

At dawn's first light, Guards of the Fifth Gate, marching:

No easy win! we've paid for this Jester
No easy win! His tilted head, his wicked grin

By noon, grey clouds shrouding the Sun, at Detention Centre C:

Drones or spells, muses the INVESTIGATOR,
his cold eyes narrowed; his half smile down-turned.

Guards, he calls, *bring me that old village spy.*

At dusk, those women of the Wishing Well:

Come all ye children, bring her locks and keys
sweet branches ablaze with a thousand bees

There's our little Abigail growing up strong
her limbs brown and golden, her hair so long

By midnight, only strands of mists swirling.

Abigail, Abigail, come to our well.
Your future, our weaving, we'll never tell.
Abigail, Abigail, come to our well.
All your lives sundered, in these waters dwell.
Where's that little Abigail, we'll never tell.

Abigail and Aunty Agatha at the Farm

HEARD OUTSIDE AUNTY AGATHA'S KITCHEN, 2058

Says Aunty Agatha to her sister Aunty Tabitha, who is stone deaf:

Hah. That thing.
Pay it no mind.
Surveillance
Drone supposed
to be hidden

And there she knits,
always the letter *A*.
And drop a stitch,
and pick it up,
always the letter *B*.

Oh, bring us the green and the gold,
                    names unknown, she croons.

Silk and cotton
Seeds and glass
says Aunty Agatha.
Oh, the air on the farm,
cheery and warm.
Not a leaf on the trees
says Aunty Agatha
our Spring is forlorn.

Aunty Charis,
long since dead,
the Book on her lap,
a pin. Not even the drone
can pick up a ghost!

WE LIVE ON JUST LIKE THAT

Every generation finds their own A!

   A is for Abigail, for Agatha, too
      crooning at night, there's our Aunt Tabitha
one after t'other, we'll now never tell
     an A to spin Fortune, her wheel be well
cardamom and ginger, parsley and sage
     imported, hoarded, and our chickens caged
turmeric and onion, our rhymes to plump skin
     we'll mend your limbs straight, smooth and strong——Bramah

throw us your Pippin File, unlock this gate
     our kitchen is calling our ovens stoked warm
        Masala stir-fry sweet honey and spice
        lavender crumbled in our copper pots,
north mixing east, west meeting south, Bramah
English Raga maid: your book full of names
      every generation finds their own A!
      Just like that.

AUNTY AGATHA'S INITIATION INTO PORTAL MAINTENANCE

In their cabin in the woods they chimed glass
stemware from the Before-Time: *Swor-off-ski*
with each toast their laughter rang out raucous.
To Good Health, they said, masks under their chins.
And a Bad Memory! Then, they fell over
giggling, coughing. One TV wire snaked
illicit Big E hookup, contraband
whisky, flavoured vapes, their eyes still clear
enough to count acorns, green leaves turning
red-edged; warming, a smoker, straw-filled skeps.
Each season, they met and said the same things.
Each decade, Earth's tilt, toward and away:
Bring us the linden tree, Bramah, they'd say.
Sweet flowers and bees to fight another day.

AUNTY AGATHA AT THE ASH TREE

Ashley of the Ash Tree
bend your branches and protect me
send your Furies, three by three
scythe and sickle, sow and owl
all my enemies befoul

Ashley of the Ash Tree
three Erinyes avenge me
smote two down, I won't frown
Ashley of the Ash Tree
all your work hide from me
mother of the three winds
Norns and Fates and Furies
iron, copper, flint and bone
to those against, your hand like stone
Janus comes, forward, back
who speaks ill of me, you'll attack

Ashley of the Ash Tree
scythe and sickle, sow and owl
loose your winds, my words do spin
Bramah sends us far and wide,
holly, cedar, oak you've seen
ruby, maple, neem and gold
from earth, in you, no dearth
Queen Kali protect me
join forces, fleet as horses
Ashley of the Ash Tree

protect all who love me
safe and strong my love's along
Queen Kali's sword up and down
Ashley of the Ash Tree
send your Furies three by three
scythe and sickle
flint and bone
your hands of stone
smote two down
I won't frown,
Ashley of the Ash Tree!

AUNTY AGATHA'S LULLABY ABOUT THE YEAR 2020

Abigail, come here. This iron hearth, this
kettle, pour; one cup for you, one for me:

I'll tell you a tale, your mother before——
    I'll tell you a tale
    in the year she were born 2020
    moths, rats, smoke drifting, a virus rampant——

Anyways, here is the butter to churn
green and golden these sticks, matches to burn.
This is what I sang her, your mother:

    In the year you were born 2020
    gases and chemicals layered our air.
    Your mother, your father: numbers who died
    Aunty Pandy swept us, laughing worldwide.
    In the year you were born 2020
    small-fisted children sent to us in care.
    In the year you were born 2020
    schools disbanded, youth gangs roamed wild and free.
    They painted red spikes, we locked our front doors
    traders resold stocks, unable to see.
    In the year you were born 2020
    Aunty Pandy laughed, her sly cruel smile.
    Come Aunty Pandy, broom held and cough
    in the year you were born 2020.

AUNTY AGATHA REMEMBERS

The year you were born, cotton, tomatoes
blocked at the border, all the planes shut down.
That Guard on the Ferry followed me home.
He come here asking a lot of questions.
I told him about all our masks handmade.
I baked him a pie, apples laced with jam.
Face to face, I laughed; flour sprinkling my board.
Them hospitals full, them gurney beds gone.
His eye on my lips, mirrored and soft smooth.
I stirred him a drink: mint and nightshade mixed.
Them fires blew south, east, north, smoke drifting—
him leaning against the sink, his gaze on mine.
Then I took him out to the Wishing Well,
his laughter unsure, his gun there to dwell.

AUNTY AGATHA TEACHES ABIGAIL TWO FARMHOUSE SONGS

Skipping Song

There's our old Aunty Agatha
Seen her walking with Aunty Tabitha
Spry and nimble, silver moon thimble

Patch 'n Mend Dig and Bend, those two
Aunties in the Pantry, honey cakes bold
Their hair so grey, their skin so smooth

There's our old Aunty Agatha
See her chat with Aunt Tabitha
Oh, those two will never get old

Race you to the Wishing Well!
Race you to the Wishing Well!

The Widow's Song

No more God, no more belief
no more husband and that's a relief
dead my dear parents, and all my children
Gather round, all my nieces and nephews
Gather round remnants and pieces
Barter me fine and barter me close
Bring me good woollens, and clean cotton sheets
silks for my handkerchiefs, and butter for my feet
Hide that one lipstick down 'neath this bed
When I die take me to the Wishing Well—

THE YOUNG DR. A.E. ANDERSON AS TOLD BY AUNTY AGATHA

At the Wishing Well, cherry blossoms fell:

Said Aunty Agatha to Abigail
that year, 2020, when she was born,
I learned again three steps forward and back,
    the power of curses to boomerang
milk turning sour—all the women on the Ferry told me,
Just you wait, Bramah will be here, but no
she never come; *I tell you I tell you,*

that seething year, teeth grinding, jaw held tight,
a bucket of doom flung, clattering
on these pebbled well walls, hard luck arrows
shooting past my hair gone frizzy with grief
the more I raged against Consortium,
    the well dried up, my hens would not lay eggs—

I tell you, Outside Perimeter, them
doctors delivering babies, her too.
What's that? Yes. It were both her parents,
took real bad by, well you know how it was—
Just a minute though, *first I must tell you*
once upon a time, many years ago
I crept to this Wishing Well, hah, young legs
bent low, my ears pinned back to hear laughter
in sunlight a string of curse words floating
into the air, disintegrating parts
each letter a bird, sharp claws with swift wings.

Aunty Agatha scratched lines; embers stirred:
    See here, girl, never let curse words
      fall on your hearth

AUNTY AGATHA TAKES ABIGAIL TO THE WISHING WELL

The Collect made us swear never to tell
never ask me whose land it is we stole—
Well anyways, we did—
register title and thus ever since
them boys brought me ashore it were all stumps
one hot July afternoon upriver
I learned real quick how to catch things and skin
rabbits, wild turkeys, salmon when they run.
Thimbleful of rice, night of no moon:
handful of salal berries, bushtit wise.
See, that's the thing, the well hides her dark eyes.
Afternoons best, overcast days, net cast,
sit still and watch, that River Woman said,
The heedless ones lay their pantries with stone.
Mind you go slow; you'll keep meat on your bones.
Anyways, doesn't make a lot of sense.
Laugh and cough, patch and mend, I see your smile.
Until Aunty Pandy sweeps in, watch out!
You'll need to marry book learning with stout.

Then she laughed long and hard, wiping spittle
her mouth two edges of torn dirty lips.

From Perimeter, women crept up the hill.
Aunty Agatha held Abigail back,
apron strings untied; a small pouch given
them settler women kept their voices low.
And Aunty Agatha did too, saying,
Lavender crumbled in our copper pots,
east west fusion mix, one pinch gets you kissed.

Later, long after those women walked home,

They brought their sorrows to our Wishing Well
we'll wash their daughters, and they'll never tell.
          Just like that——

AUNTY AGATHA GOSSIPS ABOUT HER LONG-DEAD HUSBAND

Now then now then now then, pull these carrots
oops-a-daisy, naught be lazy, pull and bend

When he bedded me, he said through his beard,
You're not getting any younger, then he coughed

I tell you; I tell you, never bake bread
when those clouds puff out their chests and hold rain

Never mind about him anyways, he's
long gone, his ashes I scattered near here

For the love of the Mother drop those sticks
Don't you know how to make a fire yet?

If money were flush, I'd put up a rock
"Never Ask a Woman Her Age, Old Socks"

Now then now then now then, pull up these beets
red and round baking, remember those sheets!

AUNTY AGATHA TELLS ABIGAIL ABOUT THE BEFORE-TIME

Outside Perimeter, huge gates, gold tipped.
We could tour their Mansions on Special Days.

Inside Rentalsman, we crammed twelve to a room.
Banned from assembly, we gathered at night.
We travelled transit to clean their houses.
We knew to remove our shoes, their front doors.
Everything we had, we made for ourselves.
Feet shod, heels worn, for sure, not rags, not yet,
toe tops scuffed. Anything soiled we took off.
Everyone scoffed at us. We just looked down.
We knew to clean them fur skins for the rich.
Well, what animals? they asked: texts sent fast.
We stitched and patched our garbage clothes, spoke soft.
On the mend, On the mend, screamed our children
from Tower Juniper, they sidelined us.

After the Second Great Banning, edicts
following quick, one after the other.
Still we gathered outside the iron gate,
Consortium approved such get-(a)ways—
What a laugh we said, in line to see
long buses deposited, a Family Day
touring to the gates, careful with our masks.
Oh, to be Conductor, a plum job!
Oh, peering into, between, faces pressed,
wrought iron and elaborate,
gold tips sharp, Consortium commissioned
sturdy locks handmade by Bramah herself.

We tracked down every rumour just to see
what day would she arrive, how to call her?
Behind bars, their verdant vegetables grew
such mellow fruitfulness, our hands trembled:
We lined up in Touring Season to see
their waterworks, their lush seedlings, ripe vines.
On the bus ride home, our children chattered
such red delight, we knew what mattered.

Everything came tiered in those days,
Tours to command higher prices.
Them who did barter butter, for eggs,
Allotment Dairies, never seen, perhaps a myth,
them that said, them that paid.
Where houses on large lots, double spread
we stood, mute, eyes downcast, cold, hands outstretched.
Those Gold-Banded passports permitted us
two hours, maximum, our children played:
Come Bramah, find us with your lock and key!

And one hot afternoon a small child ran
bones elided in that way of the times.
He slipped through iron, nimble, sure-footed
a tower child, his hair curly and black,
Vancouver Special, he cried,
having been taught the words in Tower Juniper.
Vancouver Special,
his voice echoed out over the Assembly.
Some said he were the Beggar Boy of Bramah.
Some said, his hair were fiery red.
Others just laughed and coughed,
their masks ripped and torn.

AUNTY AGATHA AND THE PARCHMENT FRAGMENT

Your mother sent me this printout, ripped, stained:

smoke concentrations may vary across
for information purposes only
pulled, viral vectors non-replicating
fine particulate matter, PM2
.5, airborne, solid or liquid, dropped
encapsulated, disclaimed landscapes
ground-level ozone, mid-afternoon winds
blowing up all along Pacifica
recombinant full-length protein strands, spiked
9-1-1 lines cut down, nowhere to hide
spring brought us sickness, summer ends burning
my microscope pieces confiscated
Outside, ragged Beggar Boys chant and laugh:
Find her chalice, don't have malice, jump, jump!

THESE CHARTS YOUR MOTHER SENT TO ME

By the order of CONSORTIUM

Release Date: withdrawn
Abstract: unavailable
Objective, participants, methods: closed.

Life Expectancy

In the year 2020	Female	Inside Perimeter	78 (in years)
In the year 2030	ibid.	ibid.	unknown
In the year 2040	ibid.	ibid.	unavailable
In the year 2050	ibid.	ibid.	35 (in years)

AUNTY AGATHA GIVES ABIGAIL A LETTER

Said Aunty Agatha to Abigail
Your mother sent this to me before she——
She kept it always tucked inside a book
She said it were from——her own mother, look:

From a Daughter to Her Mother

Inside Rentalsman, your body curved
in old flannel, blue-red stripes, soft cotton.
You carried cargo; a sister unknown.
Scolded, I ran away from you, upstairs.
Don't do that, put those away, clean your room.
All your words collided in your sigh. I
stuck out my tongue and ran up, up the stairs.
Slam! My white door shut, and you lumbered up.
Slam! Did you shake your head, I could not see.
I raced to my desk, pulled tape and paper
my brown fingers said, *Hurry, hurry.* Your
voice called my name and up the stairs wavered.
I can hear you in there! and up your gait
heavy on the steps. And behind the door
I used paper you had bought me. Scrawling,
a pencil from the twelve-pack Laurentien,
aquamarine, these gifts from you. Not-with-
standing. I wrote my message. You didn't
knock. Just paused. To catch your breath.
I heard it. In a rhythm in and out and I wrote
in a hurry. Hurry. But you needed the washroom,
and then: Slam! Click! Shut. Two doors
at the top of those old manse stairs. Yellow
and white house. You in the bathroom, peeing.
Me on the landing. I, a young Luther,

nailing my thesis. Aquamarine words
taped to my bedroom door. Slam! *I hat you.*
And you read out loud: *Oh, you've missed an e!*
Now come to tea. Downstairs in the kitchen,
saucers and cups, porcelain parts, rattle.
Upstairs, my white door creaks. My handiwork
surveyed. That piece of paper, *I hat you!*
over and over the years folded, creased.
I have smoothed out that note; up the downstairs
mother, daughter, little sister, we hold
then let go, words, smiling. Aquamarine.

THE KEEPSAKE

And here is something your mother wrote at school.
Consortium-approved, she studied hard.

<u>As submitted:</u> Abigail Ellen Anderson
<u>Grade received:</u> pass

Who said, *Write this way?*
The teacher to the student.
Who said, *I can't, I won't?*
That's what the child said
when she stormed upstairs.

You wrote, *I'll not be taught.*
I sang, *Not for long.*
We walked to our school's front door.
You read in class aloud.
I scrubbed, head down.

We slept with arms crossed
You tossed and turned and then
when I asked for dreams
you replied, *I'll write it green,*
and so we did till the end of time.

Abigail said, *Okay, I might keep this—*

HOLOGRAM MESSAGE OF DR. A.E. ANDERSON TO HER ADOPTED DAUGHTER, ABIGAIL

>>>>>>>>>>>>>>>>>>>>>>>>>>>>>>>>>>

I will be
so silent
I will be
that space
hidden
in stone,
quarried deep,
found
forgotten, discarded
found again
the stone,
thumb to forefinger—
inverted, the stone
tossed to ground water
ancient well,
hidden in a forest
the stone, igneous rock
spirals and turns
deep and drop
deep and drop, I will be
the quiet
of a forest
outside the gates
citadel city oblivious
to pine needles—
flesh of animals
after fire and ash
wind swept,
churned

still, still
I will be
the morning
long after
an ambulance cries
close, closer
this devastation:
a heart explodes,
blood in microseconds
blood without
defibrillator,
without another hand
to touch, I will be
that quiet
in the absence
just after
unseen, unfelt,
but still present,
in a hospital
in a morgue,
in an upstairs bedroom,
in a library, an office
an office
where in silence
I will etch
parchment
fingertip to stretched skin,
I will fade
with each surface breath,
brushing time,
time, deboned,
reimagined, the city
to those outer precincts
a skeleton found

outside the well,
outside the forest,
in mountains that loom at first far away
then close, closer
where the city breeds noise
but contains
dry silences
where a bird sings
liquid
two notes
dropped into morning
ice in the face of a sun
such melting, a space
and I will hang
in those pauses—
incomplete but ready
fragment of melody
singed, corroded,
punctured, long gone,
forgotten, remembered
I will be
so silent
settled along the riverbank
city with its back
to the ocean,
at night
a storefront
illumines garbage containers,
a lone seagull's
raucous appetency
Feed me, feed me,
I will be
that silent—
unending night

long after a bridge
collapses,
after tenements
tumble
water
at the water's edge
the tide carries
stillness at the edge
of sound
edged with want
　　　lap, lap, lap
water's rhythm
layered over
earth's shudder
under the water
stagnant
the well,
fathomless
forest floor braided,
extended into
the city I will be—
ever-present
a sounding line and echo
and echo, long after you've vacated
any office tower,
rooms emptied:
files, papers, pens,
long after
the last goodbye
staff dismissed,
long after
you've packed boxes,
carted, hauled, lifted,
unplugged phones,

laptop folded in half,
cellphone snapped together
shut
shut
a borrowed device,
number now defunct—
long after
you've driven off
licence plate
unknown,
home number
unlisted,
long after
you have departed
I will
be that
lonesome
ride on the road
alongside the river
where vibrations
linger east, west,
the street
more deserted,
more silent
than the emptiness drawn
from silence, full
and empty, full
and empty, I will be
that silence always
waiting and the only way
out.
>>>>>>>>>>>>>>>>>>>>>>>>>>>>>>

ABIGAIL ABANDONS THE FARM

By the hearth Aunty Agatha, her lips pressed tight.
One tear rolled down her cheek.

Down the chimney of the hearth, a thin wisp of wind.
Abigail, her eyes downcast, stirred embers with a stick.

Said Abigail to Aunty Agatha,
Well, anyway, I'm adopted so——you
can keep that long letter. Thanks for sharing.

Child, child, said Aunty Agatha, *always*
a good thing to know about the Before.

Said Abigail to Aunty Agatha,
Oh, Aunty Agatha, that's all gone now.

And with these words, Abigail of the farm
packed her bags and headed to the Fifth Gate.

Her beauty legendary, healing skills
useful. She made a living, turned her back

on fate, met a handsome Guard, hitched a ride:
transport planes running late. With Abigail

supplies never lost. No Guard smart enough
to hold her hand for long. Some said she knew

a thousand spells, some said she harboured hate:
she rarely spoke, she always drank and danced

gone by sunrise, with gold in her pockets
no matter the place, she'd dream of the well:

Making my wishes, Ma, never you tell.

The Adventures of Abigail

ABIGAIL UP AGAINST CONSORTIUM EVERYWHERE SHE WENT

In every pulsing place she saw their work
towers, prisons, agro farms without grace

Behind Perimeter, their tanks to crush
the children of migrants kneeling in dust

She learned to steal and trade secrets, her wiles,
quick-witted beauty, no one she could trust.

Purveyor of the artful dodge she missed
getting caught by a hair's breadth, just in time—

Never mind who doesn't make it, she laughed.
  Wire me and we can fake it,

        her sideways smile, her lips lifted in scorn.
        It were the year twenty-seventy-five.

ABIGAIL ACCIDENTALLY FALLS INTO A BEFORE-TIME PORTAL

i.

You white, dull-eyed, tube-bodied
eyeliner, gloss wearing low-rider
of trains and buses. You scorn walkers.
Fingernails bubble-gum pink or cherry black
chipped, grasper of small devices
emitting noise. Chatterer. You twitch
twitch in time to sound plugged into ears
tiny on your smooth head, hair dyed orange.

Tight jeans puddle narrow on your ankles
your belly rises pierced with one, two
small rings. You talk, chew, whisper
oblivious to others yet staged this drama
of indifference. A settled calm descends
on your snub features when you see me: silence.

ii.

OMG! You are so old. You suck. What? WTF!
I don't get you. Whatever. Your clothes smell.
What's with that white shirt tucked in?
I'm so excited I'm going to that concert, Tina.
Hey Devon. Get off at Metrotown, okay? OMG!
That's so cool. Did you really? I'm buying one too.
Yeah. Which? No Way. How come? Text me.
What? No. Later. Gotto go, gotta run. Yeah.

I touch my waist; then my hair under your blank stare.
Your mouth opens—a fish-maw. Some stubby energy
chews up the air around your head. The phone
a silver square. Soon you'll turn your back to me, your body
at peace in its own rhythm and I can recede
shoulders made square by your forgetting.

ABIGAIL IN PARIS

She knew how to travel invisible (translated from the French):

Outside the church, firebombed, Guards with guns.
Aided by drones, surveillance always on.

Abigail known far and wide as healer
    midwife's helper, comfrey packets, potions.
    In the Arrondissement:
those beggar children of St. Médard, called:

Abigail, Abigail
Sur le Pont
Abigail Abigail
Un coup de dés
jamais jamais

Outside on the streets, where resisters roamed.
She knew how to be in the world watching—
    She knew to trace ghost presences, the man
        known as scholar, his name whispered,
            mentioned in letters, traded in secret.
    Bartholomew the Good, some called him.
    Others, unsure, looked sideways, muttered, *Informer.*
    Outside at Rue Monge, Av. des Gobelins
    the market at Rue Mouffetard
    Jardin des Plantes, she trailed sandy paths,
    for hours she stood, the old Metro at
        Censier–Daubenton
        Square Adanson, too.

In Montmartre, outside Sacré-Coeur, she heard
that old brown Aunty, crippled limbs tucked neat
against marble steps, arms outstretched, begging
by the thinnest finger, a golden key.
Come, Bramah, sang this Aunty, *rescue me.*
Above them both on a bronze horse, St. Joan.

ABIGAIL IN AHMEDABAD

She was always eager to please, they said.
A great failing, they all agreed.

Abigail persuaded to help women
They'd come on early and wanted to end—

A great crime, you'll be punished, they told her.
She helped them anyway, without knowing
                    the nature of penalties, exacted.
Only beggar children to tell her,
                    keep searching, you'll find the way.

Find our old Aunty, she'll give you a clue.
This way, Abby-ji, for your Bartholomew!

Outside, northwest to the Baradari Gate—
A group of youths chant:

> *Her teeth were blackened*
> *Her skull were cracked*
> *Yet still she danced*
> *The Mummer's Dance*
> *No smell nor taste*
> *Let Fly, let waste*

Outside the gate, crouched low, an old Aunty
Deekrah, she whispers, taking Abigail's palm,
fingers tracing the letter *B,* electric.

(*Translated from the Gujarati by Anonymous.*)

ABIGAIL IN BAGHDAD

We said, under duress, *We might have seen.*
They said, *Find us the Green Zone,* and agreed.

We requested the necessary tools.
They would later deny this and searched us.

We maintained our innocence, despite harm.
In the end all we could point to: spray-painted

lettering, red dye, source unknown, those walls:
six strands, coal-black hair, a threaded needle.

Around a golden key, locket missing.
And said to be engraved also with these:

Q H R F

THE ENCOUNTER

She was to meet him as the sun descended,
    falling
at Down Time, they in the grove,
    accessible in those days.

He arranged to meet again,
    far from Detention Centre C.
They were intent on plants, on gardens,

meeting was about the Sun: zenith,
    when not anyone stirred,
dust in crevices. Marble.

Meeting was about the Sun:
    at dawn, the rays touching skin. An Alba.

    Meeting was about the Sun:
        absence at dusk.
Ragas to sweeten salt, the great longing
        a sutra.

And so in this way Abigail the Wanderer
bartered, traded, stored, smuggled seeds.

Point of contact
    the man they called the Good.
Unsure, she just called him Bartholomew,
    same as heard from mouths of Beggar Boys.

CALLED BY THE SUMMER SOLSTICE

Legend would say, in the years evermore
it were Aunty Agatha, sent word for Abigail's return,
pocket to Ferrier, train ride to sleeve
every note found, sent on each New Year's Eve.
What would she find there, at the Wishing Well,
an old oak box, a black leather notebook,
    cream pages, a straight-handed script:

Alas, by the time she arrived, summer—
no sign of the old oak box, just hearsay.
Passengers on the last ferry, past barges
out to the Island once were called Barnston.
Survivors ragged and few, news travelling slow.
Abigail, without expression, listened:
No trace whatsoever of that locksmith.
Abigail, her smile suppressed, looked away:
The thing is, does she actually exist?
Abigail, her eyes downcast, her head, bowed:
Some say her name is Bramah.
Some say she knows a magic spell.

ABIGAIL RETURNS TO THE FARM

فـي رِعَلْا قنَّ جَ

And brought back from her travels, exquisite
fabrics: silk damask, dupioni gold——
each one inscribed in Arabic as of old.

Come my aunties, weave, stitch new masks for me.
I've come from afar; I've crossed all the seas.

There were other inscriptions and portents.
Children begged Abigail, *Show us your cloths!*
Some said these were unlucky to open.

Come my aunties, put away your seam rippers.
This Abigail would say with a slant-smile.
At the Wishing Well, no one there to tell,

past midnight, Abigail, hair tied back, stood
six oaks encircled, acorn in one hand,
closed fist; traced by the other, the letter,

INFORMERS SENT BY CONSORTIUM

From outside Rentalsman, by the Ferry,
ragged winnower, who tore out her own tooth.

It were a time of endless announcements;
loudspeakers, no rain, a certainty.

Consortium monitored all entries, exits.
Surveillance drones, contracted satellites.

Wind whittling tiny particulates,
rows of septic-green, soldiers' helmets shone,

drill marching sergeants, troops bivouacked.
Soldiers signed up to billet at the farm.

Humped rows on city streets, tanks to crunch over
gutters oozing waste where food harvesters gathered.

Aunty Agatha and Abigail paid
piecemeal as washerwomen, harvesters.

By Ordinance, and only a number of ————

EVENING MEMORIES

We are in the farmhouse now,
writes Abigail by candlelight.

Then she writes this a hundred times:
    Before Is Also a Place.

Her handwriting slopes right,
Aunty Agatha asleep by the fire.

Outside the long summer night glows azure.

Abigail watches her pen stroke the page
she smiles at them both, stolen contraband.

Then she writes this, once, then she rips the page:

I am in the kitchen, seeing instead
    the gaze of that man they call Bartholomew
    how when he looked at me

Well, never mind, Abigail says, smiling.
Around her the air in the kitchen, waits.

Abigail tosses her page into the fire.
The house rests.

met, kissed, called, written, held, paid, given
and then you turned your back to the river
necessary fictions you told yourself.
Everywhere the signs: no one need know your
I love the way you saw in me something
Those marble floors, polished leg on leg, hands
You twisted your hips to fit that circle
I was, and you and we together cried
Cedar-scented musk at the nape of my——
Imprinted, injected, a bee, outlined
The depths of your voice that morning asking
Inside that room, inside Rentalsman, you
Your eyes, your height, your hair, always, your hands
Traced, stroked, pressed, brushed. Blackbird rising—

ABIGAIL GETS WORK AS A DAY LABOURER

That summer of '75, fierce drought.
Abigail digs the earth, at the soldiers' parade.

Abigail pretends, kerchief tied to forehead,
ahead a group of farm brigades,
women who sing out to her, smiling,

their bodies a shield,

    Because I love
to hear you call
    my Indian name.

Their voices, cover for Abigail, digging
    hidden from view, her hands cradle a phone
    cracked screen, old android, scratched with a sign,

Later, at sundown, those Guards of the Gate
against all orders, they can't help themselves.

It's the way she moves, the toss of her head
in her hands a ration card, cables—

ABIGAIL AND THE ANDROID

From her fingers a love option, slipped drink.
That Guard of the Fifth, sprawled out, mouth open.
Abigail deft, click, insert, old hub plugged.
Wires and mainframe, Big E ration on.
Head bent to the glow of a cracked screen, she
knew by instinct how to tap, pinch, scroll down.

These are the pictures, cached files swiped open:

> Always, we are bent toward my chalice
> glass slides scratched, microbes shimmering, then gone.

> Silence is a rhythm, hands, fingers teach
> thumbs swipe, scroll up, I can barely recall

> Here, this photo, and this one: his face, still——

> He works quick, kneels, large hands on newsprint

> clippings, thirty years' worth of data gone
> I dare not speak the names >>>>>>>>>>>>>>>>>

Abigail's breath, ragged and fast, she knows
this voice! Her own adopted mother, chained
to a small prison cell, face to camera.

THE LOST HOLOGRAMS OF DR. A.E. ANDERSON

Hologram #1: The Summons

Here to protect me, expanse of nation
The wild deep Atlantic way where ships once—
Estuary to river, a castle:
Bloodshed, famine, disease, those years always
Fixed distance, 2020 my birth year
And you, branded by another date, kinship
by design, not blood, was it chance or fate
Mercy knows a rock, shield, wrecks frozen,
    a bay of water so wide
Coast mountains, carved cup flowering tundra
These to keep us apart, you'd be surprised
One-sided treasure, chamber of forever
Here, I am giving you, unasked, unsought
these messages from the past to guide you
    Abigail, take heed, their powers are vast.
>>>>>>>>>>>>>>>>>>>>>>>>>>>>>>>>>

Hologram #2: Heeding the Call

Dr. A.E. Anderson, lab coat tattered
her furrowed brow, soft-strong voice vibrating—

To make the soap
To find the vials
To watch the glass

To dig the pits
To sew the masks
To find the chalice

And did Abigail turn her head away,
stolen Big E ration card, pocket jammed?

She did. Her sigh a harsh rasp, throat dry, lips
pursed, pressed, behind them the words, *Ma, I can't.*

And did she then rise, peering round the door
that Guard of the Fifth Gate, drugged, his eyes closed?
>>>>>>>>>>>>>>>>>>>>>>>>>>>>>>>>>>>>

ABIGAIL IN THE HOUSE OF THE MAKERS

In the House of Clay and Lime

They will ask me how I got here: thrown down
a portal vortex—commandeered into work,
in chains they brought me: this courtyard of stone.
Masked, we slaked quicklime. My eyes uncovered
head turned away—that dust, combustion
caustic—layers mixed with clay, to line floors
bonded brick to stone, walls, rendered, plastered.
None to know what I have seen, a future of steel.
Here, they called the clay *brickearth*, heavy
this pit lined with stones, charcoal layers, lime
kiln, to bake the ashes, that fine white powder
soon, what everyone would be after—soap—

Alkaline to wash, to cure, to make pastes
to burn that caustic soda, pH 13.
Sent to search hard woods: ash, beech, sugar maple
gathered, dried, stored, cut, stacked, those burnt cinders,
wood ash layered into a wood barrel.
First stones, pebbles, then the sweetest straw husks
to wait for the spring rains, ash soaked through,
all the while to barter, beg, steal glass jars
the ash white, eyes covered, hands gloved, hard boots
careful to bend, those chicken feathers dissolved
or a potato to float to know done!
All the things before that, stepped series, calm mind—
pouring rainwater over ash: careful!
Liquid soap to clean, to cure, a heart's full.

That tidal river, those barges and kilns
Grandmothers trekking close to river's edge
seated under a new moon, hands to sticks
to stir, sweep, brush, pour, flecks of charcoal, clay:
lime kilns fired red-hot; rough rags covered
story to task, handed down, that vast plain
where a thousand animals roamed, huge birds
lions, tigers, antelope, grasses rustling——
how they'd laugh, coughing, kneading soap paste bars
when the towers turn pink, sun's last Spring rays,

find the last glass traders: cardboard, plastic
bring us containers: ashes to our lips
once we were all together, our land joined
we can't go back though; we can't toss a coin—

In the House of the Glass Blowers

They brought before me: bowls, bottles, lamps
sand ground with seashells, hardwood ash, soda.
Before sunrise, their hands to fire kilns,
Silica lime soda, they whispered, *True*
copper measured drop by drop, *Green, ruby*
practise, they whispered, and bade me sit still
polish and grind, the years, without windows
transparent or flat enough, they then stained
story contained by lead, polish and grind
the years, until they made the bellows, hinged
container to draw in breath: expel, stoke
in and out, their fires burning white-hot.
Master of the Bellows, they'd shout and laugh:
Blow your Mould molten, fibre optics small
they made glass telescope even the stars!

They showed me obsidian cord cutters.
They showed me beads and the smallest vessels.
After midnight, surrounded by candles,
they held trembling the Sign of a Pharaoh:
They whispered Egypt to Rome, blow and mould.
They poured glazes; hot lava hardened.
They asked and I brought them, these instructions:
Millefiori, a thousand shallow vials
shaped core, overlaid colours, outer mould
pieces fused, oven baked, then ground so smooth.

They brought me to the Blowers, blindfolded.
Hours later, undraped, I could see lips
pursed over iron, mouthpiece to a knob
holding soft shapes, loaded, rolled, that hard place.
Our Marver, they called it, their tongs to lift
clip, nip, sculpt: their iron rods called Pontil.
Masked, they laughed: *We're for hire!* and asked me:
That Bramah Girl, you see her work our forge——

In the Weavers' Guild Hall

They showed me branches and twigs interlaced
warp up, weft across, their tongues clicking fast
their fingers even faster, their feet pedalling thread

twist us twine, smooth and stretch cotton, tie knots
warp up, weft across, their fingers on fire
stretch and twist before you kiss, they laughed clicking

their teeth to pull, break canvas, silk and wool
knot and lace, learn with grace: here, pull this now
batten to stuff our quilts, cross-stitch, and frame.

Our hands better than any fly shuttle
they scolded my errant fingers, clicking:
weft thread into the warp, pay attention!

Banish bobbins, forget all those machines.
Fingers weave and knot and lace, learn with grace
warp up, weft across, make your spindles wood.

Then, they led me to a darkened chamber:

⌣‾‾‾‾

Folding the edges of the mask, sides sewn.
Electromagnetic wave———front objects.
Our hands to push the fire button fast.
Hoarded, bartered, silk, nylon, cotton scraps.
Polypropylene banned, discarded, or
so said Consortium, blind eyes turning
folded fabric, half backs facing outward:
pins to pattern, quarters cut on the seam.
3-D and virtual, grooved plates, angled light
illuminations, those beams recorded.
Threaded pieces upward, threaded back down.
Reference beams, scattering telepresence:
Layered centre line, a needle and thread.
Tie the elastic and fear for our dead.

THE GUILD HALL MAKERS CHANT THEIR SECRET

At the Wishing Well we said their names loud:
banyan, oak, linden, maple, birch and fir.

North, South, East, West, each epoch brings a test.
To tie a knot, to bake unleavened bread.

To leave enough honey on the cut comb,
Come, Bramah, we then whispered, *save our end.*

From a line to a circle, spinning spheres,
spices and oatmeal, mud from the river.

Split open bark, cotton thread twisted fine,
each strand of our story woven in time.

Knives sharpened at dawn, we cut down green vines.
Sweet branches ablaze with a thousand bees.

Strike a match, light a candle, bury gold,
Come Bramah warm us, we'll never grow old.

All this they shared with Abigail and told,
Six oak trees at midnight to save our secrets.

With a toss of her head, Abigail paused
grinning, she asked, *and about that man, Bartholomew?*

Abigail and Bartholomew

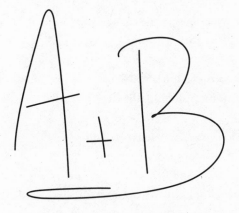

Surveillance footage to show them running—
loping gait, they stride to the lock, canal, drifters
obsessed, with payment, masks untied, hob-boots

muddied, the same path, up to the river—
snowfall, auburn pastures, stone-cutters' hut
else, city core, the Sandman, where they stayed

that night following Abigail on foot—
Later, the Boy Brigades sang, *Don't trust them,*
just call 'em, Rip Van Winkles, they coughed and——

slow walks, scythed meadows, pebbled narrow lanes
Watch your back, Abigail, you'll be wanted.
We done all our coughing, we torn off our masks.

THAT TIME OF THE WILDFIRES, ABIGAIL SENDS WORD

Ramshackle, dirt poor, fingernails broken
said strong, slow, sweet: *Only hard-luck stories.*
Lips to hands, I'll come to you in your dreams.
She said, *Goodbye to rain on the river.*
Bees encircling each breast, his name danced.
A thousand shores, those border children cried.
Shattered glass, morning's surrender, sirens
who called, the fallen on their knees, memory:
she saved six, his eyelashes, long, gold-tipped
all thought obliterated, guns drawn, hands
seven thousand kilometres, years and—
whoso serves, unlock, that gate, hair unbound
standing, his gaze sent—his last cigarette
far distances, five bombs dropped—minarets—

For calling lovers through distance and time
she knew just the spell, save he wasn't, yet.

THAT MOMENT WHEN THEY FELL

Moonlight on the bed inside Rentalsman:
Before-Time books strewn across bedsheets;
silver keepsake, golden rings, frozen fields.
Dear Dante, a thousand turmoils, distant——
Dear Zhivago, one woman's story, told.
Dear Robin, when lightning strikes, that North Shore.
Dear Buxom Girl, I seen your picture and—
Dear Wax-Jean Woman, the body promises—
To walk under starlight's infinite gaze
each moment with us emits a pulse
foretold, predestined, inescapable:
always, we are kneeling, upstairs in the—
Time smothers us in his blanket, tight-rolled.
I will sing although afraid, as foretold.

Theatre entrance scanned, each face not his—
I've started again, weeping at Seed Saver meetings,
white latex, used rubbers, after. Smoke, ash,
Port Orford cedar, built from long ago.
On stage, his hand crushed mine. There was applause.
Resistance leaders jealous of our skills.
Red is a colour on the devil's head,
refrains: outside, the detention centre—
Unanswered moon prayers, roses turned toad.
Says that quarter sphere to Venus: side smile:
night hills rise, silent snow-covered, looming,
this becoming, porous-captured, how to—
my face to his, drawn diagonal, checked.
We've come that far, driven into that wreck.

Mix recorded live, snatched, mashed, dance-hall snips.
We called it blueprint, a good ear, viral,
pitched nomadic, minus passports, easy
cluttered digital, user error, junk
bandwidths, bottled, necked out, circumference whole
tinkered with, tuned, our samples compounded.
Ah Mustafa, the women exclaimed, locked
away to the far borders, those marchers
through an open window, seen, a four-track
the way they watched us smile, we smiled back, strong
sonically squelched, suffused, captured, night
that time of meeting, the questions of where—
speak, think, make: Outside Perimeter's strike.
Our story began in Pacifica—

ABIGAIL AND BARTHOLOMEW HELP A GROUP OF SEED SAVERS

Where the fuck is he? the Guards screamed at us.
And gathered our clothes as fast as we could.
Wanted, the names of all the others.
Logged stumps, young hemlock, we chewed the needles.
Apis mellifera L., captured, chilled—
no warmth, save making, them the painters stored.
Walking toward us, silver-orbed crooner,
Bring him to me and soon: bargain pleas, worth—
less than anyone else, we would still dare
that distance, orbital range, spinning fast.
It were north in the city, ice upon—
that riverbank, his face, eyes downcast, lashed:
arms spread on the back of the wind named Niamh
my fingers, his arm, no give there, his sleeve—

Sewn inside, what looked like rips, threaded down
long past midnight, picked apart, sequoia
    red dawn, rare, seeds as thin as oat flakes
       fluttered—

ALL THE THINGS THAT THEN HAPPENED

That line where the missing-you part begins
She just wanted to make sure he lived through—
His hands on her hair, pulling. Outside, edge
snow-covered, windswept, sharp gravestone letters:
One settler: rare visits, press send, fingers—
and of that all-alone mother, no word.
Standing at the border, she wept, head raised
wall, bridge, road, checkpoint security, they
ghost workers, no airport would release the—
In the hands of the woman whose child had
that buoy, outer limits, cold dropping—
Devouring Time, where steps fell on ice
years earlier, aerial: mountain paths,
after, they realized, no one to ask—

And so in secret, no deity there
they walked to the shrine of the Kings of Laois
brought overseas from a band of peddlers

All the things not said, they'd wish them, they'd wed
melted, and loved the name, esker, and held
undulated, their song of the hollow

And threw salal down, lake basin, bowl
that moment when everything fell away
all the things not said, they'd wish them, they'd wed
and showed their palms, up, un/veined, without holes

He brought her magnolia oil, her heels chafed, cracked
newspaper lined their boots, she cried to think
all the things not said, they'd wish them, they'd wed
branded, their families, and ran, chased, outlawed
rainfall, a blanket, who could remember—

Long black strands, the past, hungry to claim her.
His fingers smeared honey, each fold, her skin.
Stop accusing me of beauty, she said.
He knew to ask nothing, that young boy's boots—
Once were warriors, they said, together.
Once fire burned, that lake, acid rain, all
things real, un/real: that resonant dance—they—
City centre, woodcut variants, inked
relief surface gouged; uncarved, reversed
by hand, each print. Door-to-door combat, press—
Machine-gunned, pockmarked walls, battering rams.
Inside, circle where they squatted or bent:
plaid shirt, jeans, heavy yellow paper, thumb—
arms up, back wrenched, eyes fixed, gun-struck
                    mouths, dumb.

—escarpment, they'd walk, slope to slope, falling
slinged arrows, sticks, guards turning over
all things left behind, they'd not tarry often

deposited on one side, eroded
steadfast the rate by which, both of them, pursued
falling, escarpment, they'd run, slope to slope
faces, a hundred thousand, captured, chained

those shadow women, who warned *Don't get caught*
those peddlers, those beggar children, arms cut
Abigail and Bartholomew, scared, still
trying to save, failing, falling, escarpment,
they'd stagger, slope to slope, ground sodden
marram grass, by seed and by root, rhizomes,
and rolled down those dunes forever and a day.

Cronos laughing, wrapped them tight, blankets!
Don't take this world too personal, prisoners said.
Doomed battles, long-shot chances, odds against,
from indifference: rapture, radiance:
And called him *beloved*, battle-scarred, who stood—
there were the demands for signs, yet none came.
There was the applause: *Then his hand crushed mine.*
They would seduce one to find the other.
Crash: symbols, timpani: borders, bridges,
men pushed barges; trees sunk in the river.
To her knees falling when called, her hair shook.
Trouble lay breathing in corners too deep.
Beauty hoarded to hide from stealing
that house, those chronic angers, no healing,

doomed causes, terrible odds, and signed—
Every last one of us, those boys sang.
In Rentalsman, they opened windows, blinds
that rapid gunfire, snow-laden trees, bent—
Surged, those after-midnight calls, therapy:
once she was Queen of all-the-street, walking.
What prisoners did and lovers, jilted, they—
With the heels of her hands, she pushed the sky,
the last scion of that lumber family.
Inside Rentalsman: heavy, soft, fluid—
Outside, bullets scavenged, melted, reused.
Months long, those battles: morning, brigades sang:
His strong hands, eyes—to want those times again,
scrapped paper, she wrote, *To have you as my friend.*

ONE NIGHT, A BARD SINGS OF THE BATTLE OF KINGSWAY

Sadness a substance, set down, front step, run—
Don't start with me, snarled a Guard of the Gate.
When they firebombed those specials, ombre.
Our gaze would always, and we found ourselves,
enough metal burned, ours hands could not hold.
Those specials, made in the Before-Time, decks,
black snake slithering, elephant heel crushed.
Pay attention! cried the tablet bearer.
Capable of, that moment on the bridge.
Look where we are brought down to, hands held strong:
blisters, barbed wire, those kinds of kisses.
She ran toward the river, knew those hills,
and called the Battle, Kingsway, us shipped in—
Outside a row of children recited—

> *Abigail, Abigail, come to our well*
> *The future's not over, we'll never tell.*

And did they then stare into the fire—
And did they understand: they must flee—

LEAVING PACIFICA TO JOIN THE RESISTANCE

Snow on the mountains, crossing the Fraser
I've put on my makeup, blanket scarf unwrapped
green wool coat on the train inside a car:
everyone quiet, blue water, white banks
gloves on my knee, phone put away, fingers—
Zhivago, you are in my brown hands, held.
City centre square, those giant reindeer—
LED lights glow silver, spun, cast, flakes
snow falling, that sequined skirt, in the court—
a drink made from tears, heart-bone of a stag:
that evening and later, these long months passed
in which the silence, with every breath, Chance—
We will meet at the Place of the Bronze Wheel.
From that treasure chest, those gems we will steal.

AS FORETOLD ALTHOUGH SHE DID NOT SEE IT THEN

Night-hours, sinews whispering to bone
Night seamstresses squatted on forest floors
Night music, feathery beats, a Snowy Owl
Each footprint, snowflake erased: a thousand
Each lamentation, hoarfrost breath, a light—
Each frozen kiss, liquid lips, stuck, melted
Shingles, spars, knot-free, ice-laden, waiting
Sitka trunk, open crown, icicle free
Silver birches, leafless, dreaming of green
Pacifica, they sang. Retreating ships—
Kingsway to Rue Mouffetard, those letters sent
They stood, market centre, each breath, a plume
They spoke mélange, crunched ice underfoot, stamped
They fell silent, long lines, those upper ramps—

TIME-TRAVELLING WITH BARTHOLOMEW

How to get used to it, the street choirs sang
Inside that room, those hooded men questioned
And so the year ended they could not hope
All her mirror-lookings, she'd break beauty
The knives stored casket-deep, just beyond reach
Destiny, Chance, Fate: these three gates opened
After the first catastrophe, the lists—
That November changed to December, risked
Supple, slender, smooth, arms beckoned, replete
Cardamom, ginger, cloves, crushed, hoarded mounds
I am here, crooned Abigail, forehead, cut
Those long-ago days, they'd kneel, heads bent low
That tension, to name/un/name, cherished, gone
And called out, moments: when he, and she, they—

FINDING REFUGE WITH AN EX-LOVER

After they cut the block, image reversed
That house, well inside Perimeter where—
Sharp sun to rise over ice-crusted streets
She studied his hands: they decided, space
Directly on the block, rough, smooth, prepared—
Outside, *Cedrus deodara*, furrowed.
North of Kingsway, Pacifica recalled.
He wrote in her book the names of artists.
London, the Before-Time, he'd retraced steps.
Every drawing, her mouth, every brush stroke—
They'd felted, carded, scraped: presence, shapes
The strength of one glance, to last forever
Outside, Boy Brigades sang: *Carmanah-tall*
Inside, he kneeled to show her, edges, all—

Untouched by language, he divined secrets
Revenant, cold-stalker, heat-seekers, gone.
Amulet, keepsake, fear-soother, held tight
his body bent over, hands adjunct, side—
Anything, is what she told him, *I'd do—*
What is mine to give, he said, *jewels, birds*
Night, a cloak of stars, morning's moon crescent
His eyes, her lips, curved, centrifugal force
Alloyed or unencumbered. Blood, bitten—
And sighed relief, machines unresponsive
To make, fall, lure, cast, hook
Corner militia, side whispers, intact
In the café, identi-fi-cation
Printed, perfect bound, encapsulation.

AFTER ARGUMENT, ABIGAIL AND BARTHOLOMEW ACCEPT A MISSION

Once lit, she was bound to watch those fires
They trekked straights, kayaked, to find messages
Mists shrouded Rentalsman, Perimeter—
Her hair should grow luxuriant, oiled
They would pull at roots: grasp, tug, twist, lift, shake—
Fall on your knees, the young boys sang outside
She bent to the mud. A single strand,
Streetside they sang: *Don't know how things will end*
Night. Woman alone, seated, her mind, limbs,
Inside, Machine as hearth, they watched TV
Imagine, she said. Of those forebodings—
Who do you read, who do you dream? He asked.
Cabinets filled with, stacks of, row upon row
Inside the Detention Centre, bent low—

And then remembered that was gone, the bridge—
After the Battle of Kingsway, tumbled
Searched salal, salmonberry, poplar-lined
Rituals supplanted knowledge; berries crushed.
Factory worker from the Place of Ribbons
Twisted paper package, sugared almonds
Seagulls flying inland, Perimeter—
The importance of self-healing, they said.
That winter the wall, unsurpassed borders
In the Hall of a Thousand Mirrors:
under bruised skin, firm flesh, opened, scent of—
Keeper of all things, the ones left behind.
Olive groves, lemon trees burnt to the ground.
A thousand memories lost, a thousand found.

THE KILLINGS

At the crossroads of the four winds, driving—
East, mink farms, poultry factories: slaughter—
There, silent entreaty, bodies hung, hooked
Woman left behind. She waded sewage—
Heart of the stag, pit of the snake, arrows
Room to room, waters rising, haunted, doomed.
Outside brigands roamed, *Am I the only*—
How to form alliances, freed from chains
Remembering the Curses of the dead.
Her brown skin everlasting, hummingbird
Although shackled, her steps resonated.
Sparrow, field mouse, rabbit, hedgehog, huddled
Inside, hours engraved, incised acid
Outside, a row of butchers, quite placid.

AFTER THE ARREST OF BARTHOLOMEW

And told no one, each silent minute stabbed
Someone, somewhere would see her, checked
              stripped, booked
Cursed eye, silver bitch, bring him to me
no pleas, vows, curses, spells, chants, prayers, or—
She would kneel before screens, ration card, bent,
their faces skulking, image to image—
In Rentalsman, snow on the park fields, moon—
those trains heading east, prisoners unbound, caught
high from the bench, the Magisterial—
gestures, these formed Omens, a bitter force.
Thousands awaited the Verdict, tanks, guns
try as she might, his face, banished, brought
that river, those hills, by Court order, she—
which were long discredited, Outside and—

Tomorrow, she told herself. *Tomorrow*—
To conquer, to come in from afar, he'd
mandrake-root dug, one long emitting pulse
self-healing, well within Perimeter
seclusion-distance, enemy-friend, they'd—
nightfall. A number of explosions, cries
skin, bone, his hips against, each—and pounded
a new kind of war, those border journeys.
In the lab after the Fifth, they pulled at—
he'd stood at her back, raised her leg and then—
Every café, market square, riverside—
tunes played for cover, honey smeared, knives, drawn.
In time, she'd come to understand, sharp-soft
a long line of women marched hands aloft.

His face upturned, eyes: centre, square, plaza
A meditation on incompleteness—
Underground basements, archival papers
The story of his family dispersed to—
All the questions I never asked you, she—
His voice, a sounding: river, ocean called
She remembered his slant smile, their kisses.
Midnight car, parked, door open, her knees, moss—
he gripped her arms—roaming militia, lights
They'd made love under threat of danger, then
Consortium directed their actions
Pacifica, as then were called, riots, guns—
A thousand names, the Fraser, the Shannon
Come again to me, she crooned, abandoned.

ABIGAIL CONTEMPLATES DIVINE ASSISTANCE

Those gods, their terrible laughter, and watched.
Early morning trains. Mist in the valley.
Woman walking alone head uncovered.
Untuned piano, lid closed, songs captured.
The hare limped trembling through the frozen grass.
She wrote inside Rentalsman, *Dear Bramah*—
Durga, Kali, Ruth, Evangeline, all—
That they might bring, her worn shirt, shoulders thin
Lived, loving luxury, comfort lost, called to—
Assembled each day in the courtyard
Would wait for light: shades deepening, head raised
Fingers to parchment, Sanskrit-braille: fan-shaped—
Called the Six, the stench of them heralded
Red cottonwood boiled, sin-sweet resin grasped.

ABIGAIL WAITS OUTSIDE BARTHOLOMEW'S PRISON

Star-crossed they stood; a week's worth of glances
Centre disintegrating, margins, guns:
Alive, those long lines, a border, a wall
Perfumed wrist, ankles, cinched waist, his fingers
And travelled the whole world over, they sang
And stood frozen outside that northeastern
Trains sounded their metal-on-metal sighs
Painters, printmakers, joined their materials
Stretched, the animal skins hung, scraped, dyed, cured
Her one-year sentence and beyond, counting
Seven hundred miles, that wall, those fences
In the bar, that Guard's knee pressed close, sirens,
Brigands, brigades, agents, spies, drones, cameras
Aerial, more than fifty thousand. Borders—

ABIGAIL SENDS WORD TO BARTHOLOMEW FROM THE WARS

To keep faith, to row against the current
And knew you would and said so, before we
Robbers, outlaws, fugees, militia, they'd
Posted, your photograph, the two of us
Your breath warm on the back of my neck, when
I made things sewn, painted, handled rejects
Outside, those eight skeps set on fire, names
All the ways you'd take, and me, receptor—
Linden, locust, long rows, the river, bees
Your gaze, touch, briefest taste of—I'd never
Moments after those five explosions, glass
Shattered, dreams of a nation, war without
Endings, *I am writing to you my love*:
I am fated to travel these Portals——

Waiting for the snow, she called him by name
herself, woman running away from fate,
she with familiars, Seed Savers, who'd help.
Her radiance, a calling card, doors opened:
beauty, that firepower, ice melting
to bear image, she whispered his name, secrets
past midnight, before dawn, she'd lift her hair—
This were the time: Great Register, guards, scribes
fields abandoned, aprons, tattered edges.
Their gear stolen, incarcerated, marked
behind closed lids, she would see again, his—
Two combatants: muscled frailty, the Book.
She knew his arrival, heads turned, each look
Outside, a thousand tanks, guns turned east——

ABIGAIL SEARCHES THE SECRET GARDENS OF PARIS

Those endless days, no way out, no escape.
To wake and look up on green, living things—
Parking lot to hotel, she spoke his name
Each person a magnet, attract, repel.
The Night of the Fifth Bombing, she would search
I just knew, you'd choose her, not me, she said.
That room, the three of them, hours, image—
Painters, printmakers, potters, weavers, all—
Crushed almonds. A cup of sugar, stolen.
They'd stashed her letter in the Bakers' Guild
What a terrible time to be alive!
Those Brigades crossed rivers: *Jamais, jamais*—
Smuggled house to house, angled, those brushes
at midnight, sweet trills, the Song of the Thrushes.

Chained, they said, *what we can build together.*
Really good-looking men, seek me, she—
Years, they said, *no speech between,* stolen, given, found
Did I ever tell you the story of—
Damp, quivering, she shook, recalled, how he—
Eyes, glances, the power of, across space:
Paris, Square Adanson, they stood, that tree
Plant names, bees, a garden; painters, potter's wheel
Discarded digital, her eye, dead girl—
In the Great Hall of the Palace, framed face
A thousand rubies, Perimeter clasped.
River barges towed; mills emitted smoke.
Effluent ridden, they dredged deep to find and
Those many severed hands, *un coup de dés*—

ABIGAIL RISKS A MEETING WITH THE BUTCHER OF PARIS

Maple stick in hand, she knew to churn sand
X marked, dug, to call for the names, one thousand—
That bridge across the river, bodies thrown
Christmas Day, in the year of the reign—they—
The Sun rose, crowds assembled, Rue Mouffetard
silent, full force, rays golden, the unburnt
That long drape, Trouble's cloak, when he knocked on
doors opened, shut. Would she still dance when the—
Of that necessity, no one could see
Woman running away from Fate, she bent
legs shackled, she stood in the plaza, chained
Left-Behind Mother, chair-bound, her body—
Impossible to know which hour, the last
Two candles lit, snow falling, Time's hand cast—

In the Théâtre de la Huchette, staged
We think of you often, she wrote and trust that—
Foot ferry to the Island, rough waters,
Consortium directed those planes sent
A hundred survivors in the basement.
Out here everyone demands smooth, he said.
Un/inhabited, she went to paper
and spoke, that painting, hunters in the snow.
Up along the coast, his father once, his—
Un/couple, unbend, unlock, if only
She'd come through, he vowed, blood-rushed,
ice-stung-sharp—

And would have seen before, fur-racked, aflame
legs crossed, arms extended, a thousand names.

IN AHMEDABAD, ABIGAIL SECURES A RENDEZVOUS

You put yourself out there, you will be judged.
Old friend from far away, the women sang.
His fingers splayed, that paper, imported.
Stern Warden in the Prison of Roses
sat, silence, a hundred strands of hair.
That moment when, and then, then: tied, unbound—
Constant confessional, devices employed
the heel of his hand, the crown of her head:
Lakhan, ghost rider, Railway red juncture
they'd moved on, left town; she'd remained, writing—
On this day, fifty years ago, she wrote
think on all you love and call them closer—
Heart of the stag, tears of the lion, this—
Oh little sister, fate twists and turns—

Letter-writing, reading. Conjure-connect.
When had they built their nests, those three *Hav-las?*
From long ago and far away: scripts, scarves.
Those Tabla players found her, night seamstress.
Called Penelope or—Scheherazade—
Creating the illusion of comfort:
Flannel scraps, one lemon, pot of honey.
Stirred ghee, to soothe a prisoner's hands—thumbs,
concoctions heated without electric.
This woman who thrived on adoration.
Inside Perimeter, inside the Lab,
blood spun concentric; sugar cubes melted.
Those women armed, a decade of fighting,
Jaldi! Memsahib, they urged, sighting her.

Truth: she did not know how to be, this world
hunger unresolved. Caged, children hung, mute—
The Pelt Broker promised to give her news.
Alive in her body, broken, those dreams,
clay thrown, wheeled, paint, swirled; outside, men crouched low
so that one task might flow to another—
She ran the hill called Mistress Jitali.
Beggar children chanted, *Abby-ji, come!*
Thereafter to ease, she would cede the field.
Help her, the beggars sighed. All around them,
Stick to the plan and don't go fey, they warned.
Young girls blossoming everywhere, soft skin
Change: enough to rip them apart, jagged—

Ice-fed, snow melted, a bucket of stars,
In the hour before sunrise, three notes.
Yes, you will find him, foretold the Mother,
garden-recreated: *Generalife*
Divining wheel, a thousand threads entwined
named *Al-Hambra*, she knew to expel shame,
hidden: Cascara girl: camas lilies, pine.
Woman, drifting Outside Perimeter—
Woman on a platform waiting, eastbound
Sometimes his absence settled upon her
Sometimes every key thrown, every gate locked
forward, backward, a thousand clues gleaned.
Badari Gate fortune teller, palms stroked—
His eyes downcast, cuffs, embossed, cut, revoked.

IN BAGHDAD, ABIGAIL DEEPENS HER SEARCH

His touch, a firepower, a light burn.
Star-crossed, they'd not meet for months, travelling
black, white, those squares alternated, endless
through that battle hand to hand, they'd danced
her foot on the last loom in the city.
Outside, banned from Guilds, year one, a gift:
Borrow, beg, rob and steal, that's our meal, they—
Her left side: ankle, knee, hip, wrist, face where—
Those curses handed down, mother to child
silk pillowcases where her cheek rested
his height, shoulder to waist, a ratio loved.
She would return, those books, saved scrolls, margins
at night, forests patrolled, *Morus alba*—
Various species held at Zafraniya.

Cruel cold winter moon, wolf-eye and sleek.
Each day plaited, engraved, stamped with longing.
Queen of the Night, she walked those rooms, no one—
Her quest for clues, prisoners moved, month to month:
Green Zone soldiers smuggled news, notes crumpled.
Grotto, cave, altar, woods: to search for and—
In the name of the dead heroes, she said.
She knew he would—print words raised to touch, rough,
gold pendant, heart-shaped, black silk thread, frayed.
Struck down, killed, that instant, birds rose, gliding—
How did we rise, conquered, rising again
And went for him, into that bitter wind
Who will we be, when taken and every—
Could only weep, memories sweet, sharp, savoury—

For weeks that Moon shone down.
And then cried as they ripped her garments, thrown
overboard, excess, in that age, everything
severed. And wanted for nothing: birds, seeds.
The soldier who forced her never mentioned—
This power of what they witnessed, written,
scrolled, intricate, curved, filigree, inlaid—
They said of her, *She won, lost, hid her scores.*
Coal-black face and limbs, forehead, that wood rubbed.
Carried, trucked, grabbed, kissed, Paris to Baghdad.
In the memory stories of the Aunties—
Money spent, to study absence, Seasons—
To then awake, snow falling, city lights,
And unspoken, his name, a thousand nights.

On the battlefield called Forever, they—
His hair, the women sang, *the colour of*—
From that moment on, she asked, *What happened?*
A series of interrogations. Night.
They rode those waves: riptide, reef, breakers.
His hands, both sides of her waist, where bees danced.
Fourteen sequins, sixteen threads counted, called—
At the corner of, within pistol range
after he—she thought of—and wondered if—
Beyond the fortified wall, that city
Designated, set apart, who was, and—
Confiscated: thin, narrow, flat, his tools.
Safranine, dyed wool, silk, their stories, spooled.

Her intent, destruction, those two girls, kept—
Days, from that moment on she lived, snowbound.
Voyages, overland treks, trails, tears, ships—
That Register, inventory, famine,
O for the sun, those far plains extended.
And wasn't she always on the outside.
Look in, said Abigail, *and jump*, eyes closed.
At the gates of the city, blistering—
Beleaguered, that North Wind: rubies, emeralds.
His mouth, his eyes, hand to grasp—paint, brushes,
Hologram soldier, riverbank scrub, dug—
Balut, her nickname, a grove of Tamarix.
For these she would, and did, the most to risk.

Those war heroes, damaged, who called to her—
Women standing, faces raised, their cameras
an endless series, posed she would name them.
When days later, they found the girl, Number—
If a mother, I'd teach children to dance.
Each inscription, skin injected, black ink
prepared surfaces as indicated.
Outside Rentalsman, a man screamed: voice, raw—
She would worship rain, coolness before ice
each girl stood, feet encased, newspapers torn.
Abandoned, the lab where once traces found
they would wake, dreams hollow, filled with others
un/birthed, un/sought, nevertheless, longing—
His first year served, a thousand days remained.

ABIGAIL INDENTURED IN THE BEE PALACE OF BAGHDAD

Tissue gampi & the Scimitar, sang
those slave girls, as they taught Abigail too.

This off-white, neutral pH, machine-made
strongest, that plant fibre, searched for, and grown
thin, lightweight, shiny-translucent. Banned, loved:
Torn surfaces, mended. Bee upon bee—
Over a hundred million years, his lance
to cut, clawed or straight-bladed, honeyed steel.
She would hand-cut stamps onto sheets, the bees—
Together, they would make-unmake, he said:
Lost, those words, having been held, divine lips
Under that cross-hatched, armed citadel, stormed.
A hundred straw skeps burned, those armies, black
Persephone, Thanatos, although unverified
Printed sheets, demi-silk, tactile and pinned—

Hand to hand, mouth to mouth, each night a tale.
This the slave girls warned Abigail to do:

to begin, begin timbre, velvet voice
to begin, begin texture, soft supple
to begin, build: slender ankles, arched heel,
don't forget about your intellect—
to build, build muscles, taut calf, pliable strings.
She conjured in between someone, no one
that rise, full, swollen strong below, waist, hips,
and above circumference, point seven, small
Barbie from Before: now, Kali, warrior
Triceps cut, shoulder bones showing, long neck.
Outfits assembled: clasp, hook, match, made-in-
the Bee Palace, Resistance women, kept.
Mistress silver, golden chains encircling,
story night by story, remarkable—
Scheherazade.

ESCAPE FROM THE BEE PALACE

She lamented not keeping one strand, of hair.
Haunted forever by his deep laughter.
rumbling migrations, Old Quarter tiles stroked.
Gunshots, cash registers, a fisher-woman's chant
spliced into, and inside, those squares, that hall.
She would run to him, despite, and unseeing
ghost towns, those lines and borders, towers built
jangled, jagged, that Paradise forgotten.
The sheen of her hair when taken, head bent
his shoulders, his jacket, dark-blue wool, found
wood rationed, every stick burnt, they would hunt
those children with words ink spattered, plangent
heard faint, dusty corners, blind alleyways—

You know you're in trouble when this, written,
warned, a threat; renewal prohibited.
Lips, eyes, her scent, waist to hips, a ratio—
ever after on the twentieth and—
faded, a softer shade, worn, washed, women,
again and again she applied colour—
She knew she'd be punished—a matter of—
O sun who shines, just, unjust, bone-breaker
outside Perimeter, head bowed, eyes down,
raised curious, she got up again and,
her grief in each home; outside, children, played.
She knew never to; street corners, guards roamed.
In the city, after—woman, alone.

BATTLES AND DEPRIVATIONS

Hedonistic rituals to forget, else—
They did not speak much, ephemera-glad,
he, a bad man, rising, walls, borders—
This madness surrounds, they whispered, sighing
Yes, we want what we can't have, they murmured.
Stories: lost, embroidered, stolen, bartered.
Monarchs to land, her arms bare, glistening.
He'd hold her hair, while she would, forbidden
arid the months without music, dancing
clenched, pummelled, grabbed, gripped, his into and she—
Outside Perimeter, wounded prisoners.
Her cheekbones, lips, breasts, hips, rosewater, dabbed.
Each scrap, paper passed, hand to hand, long lines
dust, scorched fields; ice, the city, those far chimes—

Dear Bartholomew, Abigail recites
although I've been unfaithful, I still search
    for you.

ABIGAIL SECURES BARTHOLOMEW'S RELEASE FROM PRISON

Squandered, the camps, a blacksmith found her name
imprinted, those spurs, hunt, rowel, straightened
teeth cut; rims parallel: the word went out.
They would bring fireside, evergreen leaves
etched in blood, sandpapered, still legible
Daphne laureola: he painted, brushed
stroke-upon-stroke, blended, smudged, eyes downcast,
winnowing fork, tuned, he bade her stand, stared.
Shoved out by the Guards, she ran to him, kneeled.
His golden cuffs were magic, he told her.
Papers folded, a potter's wheel, clay, ink—
Midnight, on a train heading east, cold rails
The way their eyes looked up, locked in, held fast.
Their fire unquenchable, his hand, hers.

Songs, secret gardens, hidden names, fresh snow
metals, silver-golden-topaz molten
his hair, that colour, long over shoulders.
Her full lips parted, to take in, nectar
dead bees, *Apis mellifera L.*, skepped
condo to condo, Tower Juniper.
From there, she was led to a prison cell.
Barrios, that un/named girl, guns, a flute
those trees, honey locust, branches breaking.
Labyrinth entry, he'd found her, they would—
Her name, his voice, asking—every border
Perimeter checkpoints, disguises, covert
in the park, a table, bodies opened:
Cut, mend, snip, sew; that kiss, a thousand sighs—

ABIGAIL AND BARTHOLOMEW REJOIN THE RESISTANCE

Guadeloupe to Pacifica, stored
dismembered, reassembled, Toronto
Paris, Théâtre de la Huchette: shrine.
Such a long journey, Ahmedabad, circle
inside Perimeter, Baghdad: bound, kept
her limbs mahogany-painted, rubbed, oiled
those eyes to see, veiled, a thousand lips, touched,
opened, those throats parched still quenched singing, *come.*
They counted sixty-four explosions: night;
descended: powder, rags, crowds gassed, dispersed.
Inside that walled compound, he painted, lines
fragrant, her presence everywhere, he said.
Although never kept, unheeded, she wept.
They would interconnect, across space, time—

ABIGAIL DISPUTES THE FINDINGS OF A STRAY ORACLE

Something from nothing: they built those houses;
Three-ply, no chlorine used, bleached, bio-de-
Shift workers, factories—girl gangs and after—
Sent east to a youth camp, Seed Savers banned.
Living through new wars melded to old wars.
Last seen walking with those two informers.

All your letters to him will be waylaid.
El-Khemi: spinning wheels, machines, his face.
You may think you can avoid joining but—
One envelope, two photographs, your child
from this journey, quite by chance, you will drown.
Composition, the frame of the picture,
the father of the child killed in battle
those lowland woods, hidden amid cattle——

GUARDS AND INFORMERS TRACK DOWN ABIGAIL
AND BARTHOLOMEW

In those times some would write, some, never—
And lifted that calf overhead, until
The Tale of the Last Matchstick, she—
Not there, in the ground empty, stone cold, not there
Morning: small tasks, to light a fire, cook food
Images of their faces, circulated
sectors, districts, Kingdoms: Perimeter
by the light of two candles, her fingers
as she sat by the woman's bedside and—
Let, how, so, that, this, then: within each, once
He trudged along train tracks, whistling those tunes
Although cut, immobile, still should, could, count
the names of the months, what once they called years.
Laughter resounded, no warnings, no seers.

At the March of a Million Women
Abigail and Bartholomew gave slip to the Guards.
And Time, their great enemy, looked away—

ABIGAIL AND BARTHOLOMEW ARRANGE A SECRET MEETING

Platform, our parting glance, emanations
thigh against table, folded newspaper
red, white, that cloth, plaid; my face upturned, you—
locked gates, city on fire, we fled, turning——
Outside Perimeter, park's edge: checkmate
that potter's wheel, white buckets, secret codes.
Bramah, bring your lock and key, those boys called.
From Tower Juniper, the seer said. *Run*—
In the library, a thousand copies.
Dark, coming in early, they marched, shackled
and recalled Before-Time movies, threads—
nail-studded, shack-door, and could not believe.
Speak, speak, speak her names, black-haired, full-lipped.
We would stand in the shadows, smoke drifting—

All that winter she kept herself in wait
Fleeting moments held a long time, he wrote
not the Good-Bye River, not the town of—
smokestacks, that room, polished where Time measured.
They would lie undetected, closer to—
he sat, circle's edge, sound permeated
his compositions: music, paint: notes, strokes
she walked Perimeter, counting bees, birds.
That Night Militia rounded up dozens
snow muffled, the trains, east to west, shunting
try as she might, they would, nonetheless, come—
Buckthorn, beeswax, rose, lavender: fingers
They would carve his name, he would fold, revive
That centre within, he made her alive.

ABIGAIL CONCEIVES HER CHILD

And our great enemy the Sun, a star:
heartbreak, a way, paths of tribulation.
Winter Letters: *Dear Bartholomew*, you—are
the most beautiful man I've ever seen.
Our wayward ways, our loving ways, come back!
I love the sound of your pencil on cream paper.
In the Room called All-Spice, lemon peel steps.
Two moons foretold that night, dull knives, chilblains—
We had found charms once, on Tamboline Road,
Girls, if from Tower Juniper, were to—
We knew nutmeg, if mouldy, were poison,
means to light a fire, boil water, soft rags—
My cervix dilated, we held hands, breathing
that cherry-red coat, that open field, meeting.

ABIGAIL AT THE LAKE

Nine months in, no mirror: just this deep lake
Spring Equinox, where once Sakura——

blossoms, each petal a foretelling, if——
only these black strands were soft enough to

unwind around my fingers each moment
that time we lay under a fat pink moon:

Oh, you will return to me while stars turn
I am stepping over that threshold and then——

Now, there is no one to sing of battles
barricades thrown open, Perimeter:

vast encampments on this spinning sphere, torn
atmosphere burning, radars tuned northwest.

We were asked to find our people, to stay
indoors, an unquiet rest, endless days——

TO THAT WHICH IS TO COME

10:30 a.m. and a Saturday
Love's sudden arrival or disaster
Bam! Outside Perimeter, inside, his—
Rentalsman, where the two of them, lying
His voice, the strength of his, foundations shook
Cadmium red, ultramarine blue, pulsed
Those Girl Gangs, longed for, belonging-laughter
Things quickly got out of control, she said
All-the-Times-Gone: resisted, imprisoned
Those desires came upon them: colours, songs,
Five-fingered those options, they ran out, robbed
What did she want most in this world? he asked.
Broken those rules, to be remade, singing
words repeated: acorn, agate, healing—

They knew their fate and yet chose otherwise.
Guards of the Fifth made sure they could not kiss.

>>>>>>
👑👑👑

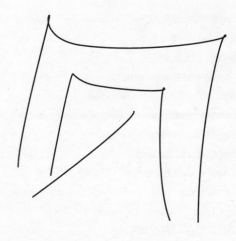

Each blossom petal stunted on each branch
forerunner: war without end.

Roaming deserted streets, girls sang letters
spin, rotate, tilt and orbital, our Sun—

Find us Sakura, bitter pink, rough bark.
Come ye, Aunty Pandy, sweep and cough.

Our spring is our autumn, falling leaves fall.
Indoors to outdoors, gathering us all.

Spin, rotate, tilt and orbital, our Sun—
Green is our golden, acid our rain, falling
        who do we long for, her keys large and small.

Outside, drupels and red berries——————burnt flowers,
Inside, in prison, Abigail counts——————hours.

THE LETTERS OF ABIGAIL AND HER LOVER, BARTHOLOMEW

As surrendered to the INVESTIGATOR:

Migrant Camp #3

Dear Bartholomew,

I am writing to you against the night—
really, we are part of everything Before and After
Tilt and Spin.

I found this on Cy-Board #6:

Harsh tilt they couldn't steady it, hot and cold
The women at Patch 'n Mend just laughed—coughing,
Find us a packet, oh find us a packet of soap

I am writing to you, night phobia increasing
waxed, waning, each hour reduction, grey
fog waters moonlight, my words reach—

their ultimate destination: by turn, solstice,
equinox, each threshold a portal

Long ago, you and I in——
That was the time of times
and then, and then—

Love, Abigail

As confiscated by the Guards of Fifth:

Migrant Camp #8

Dear Abigail,

Where are you this month,
this day of the month, this year?

Everything was once horizontal:
a car park, double garage, acreage, a hobby farm—

Everything then
went vertical,
cramped up and down,
unit-living. When Aunty Pandy struck
why, we just couldn't———

I remember those little shops,
to be with you again, to drink tea and talk for hours,
low ceilings, greasy cutlery, threadbare carpets.
I remember how hard I tried not to look at you.
Looked instead, at the bones in the hands of the server,
only later, into your eyes. Abigail.

And now—
I remember fresh crisp Autumn air.

Within Perimeter,
outside Rentalsman,
on the appointed hour,
we are allowed to harvest rain
and test for burns.

Missing you, X

Bartholomew

As intercepted by the INVESTIGATOR:

Migrant Camp #3

Dear Bartholomew,

Do you ever miss the taste of blackberries?
We camped out that night in X——

Mid-range hotel, you recited every poem you knew,
your fingers lifted a length of my hair, lips whispering,
Blackberry blackberry.

Yes, my lovely long absent B.
That night in X, your words like wallpaper
standing naked before me, back to the mirror,
afternoon light: Zukofsky's flowers, Pessoa's disquiet.

Library, you told me, miming, your hands in the air
the shape of an old hard-bound book.

We counted syllables together.
Our eyes closed,
we saw the earth, then, as green——

I still haven't given up hope
A funny thing. Feathers and so on.
Night groans with memory.
Once you were as a boy with me and I——

Without you, the night is no friend.

Love, Abigail

As Misdirected, holding zone, Outside Perimeter

Dear Abigail,

Yesterday, down by the river——they have us now in work gangs.
Or, was the place, oceanside,

that Pacifica, harbours closed,
Harbourmaster imprisoned, any number of containers,

bleached, migrant communities,
militia not bothering, small shack where once the fishers,

I saw a group of men and women,
fingers on a scarred concrete table,
gesture as if writing, heads bent, swaying left to right—*Come, Bramah,*
    they chanted—

Around the dock, faded in grey, pallets, skeps of straw, gasoline soaked.
No one with a match.

A woman threw a bouquet of dried grasses,
she said, *There are no Beggar Boys left here*

to remember the names, to call the chants
to bring the spell, to unlock the gate.

Come Bramah.

I hope to see you again, Abigail.

(If this reaches you, pay the courier well
his looks I fear, his intentions I doubt).

As ever, I am yours,

Bartholomew

As confiscated by the INVESTIGATOR:

Migrant Camp #8

Dear Bartholomew,

Today would have been your birthday. I feel sure of it.
I haven't heard from you in so long but still wanted to write.

Again how strange the workings of Consortium.
To still get mail!

I wanted to write words my aunty taught,
from memory. Or, what we learned in that philosopher's book

gold and green, seen up on the highest shelf
stolen goods stacked in the Militia House:

I will write here on foolscap,
gift from, well, yes, there, I must say it, a guard.

He tells me my hair reminds him of a blue-black night.

Happy Birthday darling:
as though everyone served
as though illusion that death
as though all the books before
as though all these melodies
all this stored Time————

Love, A.

Dear Abigail,

In the church at Aleppo, machines cut
all their paintings. Let this letter be sealed.

Al-Shabab! Bring copper or iron.
Not authentic. Check online while e-pulses
still available. Everyone's private generator.

And to Pacifica, then we came—shipped.
Containers: ocean-going, from Japan.

Separate, corrected for, spherical
Apocope, the name of our familiar

treasured. Rejected by most authorities—
authenticity, doubtful. Hidden, unknown, spurious

happiness, fleeting, amid fear to find
talismans, ankh, tablet, pocket treasures.

Such omissions spoke to us of rhythms
loss borne in the cut of—

Each letter of each word, the peeled core
    Inside, were syllables

with each month, less able to speak
only here, alone while paper and pen
still given

angled, language found its way,
outside, to inner compartments.
Your coal-black hair, your glossy brown skin.

X, Bartholomew

As held by the INVESTIGATOR, three letters:

Migrant Camp #3

Dear Bartholomew,

Yes. I am pretending everything did not happen.
I woke up humming:

Find our old Aunty, she'll give you a clue
This way, Abby-ji, for your Bartholomew!

Before is also a Place. I've lost count of catastrophe.

Our town lies dying in disarray,
infrastructure decayed.
Buildings sink, tilting and torn.
Ceilings sag.

Power lines, downed. Roads buckled and split.
Sidewalks caved. No central heating anymore.

We haul polluted water, metered out from the river,
armed guards keep watch.

Myriad DIY and clandestine operations flourish halfway up the hills.
Water purification is busy business.

Those townspeople who figure out a way to purify the filthy water
charge exorbitant fees for tiny amounts and we do drink these.

City trees, hoarded, chopped for firewood.
Consortium decreed all of us:
    A Workers' Brigade of women
      yet still we weep streetside, feet bandaged in rags or barefoot,
each time a mother root ripped—

Loving you always, Abigail

Dear B.,

Nights I chronicle.
Days I survive.

Confession: so lonely my limbs they find strangers,
or imagine, fingers——

River women provide a brisk trade:
expired contraceptives and balms,
pots and jugs of wax, rancid butter, too:
   for bruises.
Just like those women of the Wishing Well. Ha!

All services, from medical to electric
hook onto one grid, Consortium-controlled.
Set hours, on a charge basis.

Conscripted, doctors, nurses.
Everyone trades, barters, sells,
   cheats, lies, steals, hoards.
We've our bodies and remembered skills.

They keep the sick and the infirm outside, too.
Not the aunties, though. And a few Old-Timers.
Resilient! Thrifty, they sew, darn with needle and thread,
Flour or whisky made from anything!

There's a brigade of them called Patch 'n Mend:
my paper and pencil suppliers, running out, of course.
Last winter, Aunty Pandy hit us hard, surging——
I did miss you, then.

I am resolved to write,
no matter what happens.
Inscription tools and surface material:
I think about these a lot.

Dear Bartholomew,

——limited electric-hours, rationed,
my pass digital, Consortium-approved.

Barter! Radio and TV, broadcasts twice daily.

Weather reports best from the Patch 'n Mends:
each morning we go outside,
sniff the wind, test direction,
check for Burning Rain marks.

No one wears masks.

A few homes still stand Outside Perimeter,
usually rented:

here we barter, sell, cadge phone calls, pick up mail:
the phone lines, totally Consortium-controlled.

I've not seen a cellphone in ages——
Mail is often hand-delivered,
tower to tower and takes months, even years.

Today, at the Fifth Gate, those Guards, their room
where we all sign in, Consortium-approved,
my eyes alight on a shelf of books, then
quick, sweat on my wet forehead, I looked down
my gaze on the gun, propped against the wall.

Each night up at the Wishing Well we hear:
Mind you never make eye contact,
Them's the ones that want in return:
favours——and then the old ones laugh and cough.

I am forever yours, A.

Dear Bartholomew,

Third Trimester Dream:

pleasure an intensity to find, break
    midway, between carpels, separating,
gynoecium silk tissue gampi and
    thirty thousand bees
    waxed.

Dear Bartholomew,

I love when my ways find me,

Do you remember Aunty Agatha——
    those long summer days when seasons were true,
seated across from dusty migrants, weaving,

We must meet for sixty-four afternoons,
at eight p.m. precisely, each Thursday.
This were the first catastrophe, I think.

Set testament down, she instructed.
And we, all dutiful:
Listen, there will be fear-gods everywhere.

Do you remember her small strong brown hands——
nails short, square, vestiges of pink paint, smoothed

paper squares brought in on her way, ordered,
off-white, neutral pH tissue:

Overlay the story, interweave parts, she said.
We all nodded, pretending to understand.

Perfect for mending, she laughed, her voice hoarse.
We sat side by side and did not wear masks.

At night, hands on my belly, her words speak,
Consortium-approved; midwives just laugh.

I will write to you in any way I can,
your loving Abigail

Dear Abigail,

—from the edge of the encampment known here as—
Doctors recruited, worked to death, or shot anyway.

A woman said to me:

Yes, after he paid her for sex the second or third time,
he, under kidnap, famous, others called him a great writer
Je n'aurais rien à regretter

The children of the camp sing, *Been so long.*
At dawn, sweepers chant, *Jump the fence.*
They speak it real soft and slow, brush, sweep, brush.
At noon, during inspection, the children
call out, voices parched from lack of water:

Hey Barth-o-low-mew
Hey, You Haven't Got a Clue!

I smile at them with their French, Cantonese and Gujarati.
You would love them all.

There's an old aunty here, wizened, stooped low
smooth brown skin though. Sparkling eyes, she laughs, slant,
turns my palm upright, slowly shakes her head.
If you send word, she'll know where to find me.
Tomorrow they transport us, the next camp
infiltrators tell me, Cy-Board #6, tracked.

Past midnight, echoes linger,
Un coup de dés, jamais, jamais

And I agree.
I am writing to you always and a day,
no matter what,
I am yours,

X. Bartholomew

From Migrant Camps to the Stone Marker

AS RECOUNTED BY THE SOLE WOMAN SURVIVOR,
MIGRANT CAMP #3

They made me get rid of my red tattoo.
This is what it said:

(translated from the Gujarati)

Those things that sought the light:
I threw them into a bin of darkness

ગુજરાતી લિપિ

I bartered food for this Tale:

The last place you'd want to go is here: *Run!*
Our Grotto, shrine ransacked, icons strewn, gold
And knew no other place to turn, corners
On your knees, they will open your lips: *talk.*
In Paris, that printmaker of Baghdad
Those brigade boys chanting, out of sight, mind
Blanket to blanket they slept under signs
The Road to Ahmedabad, buses filled
Historical, a method: tied, placed, set
Blank Time, that terrifying space, between
And headed to the old cemetery—
Perimeter, City Centre, rubble
They'll gouge her eyes, that far shore, windy beach
Woman alone at the end of the world.

We called her Abigail.

AS HEARD AROUND THE MIGRANTS' CAMPFIRE

They say she arrived at the sound of the Beggar Boy chants:

> *right as rain*
> > *good as new*
> *c'mon Bramah, give us a clue!*

Huddled corners full, those child conscripts kneel.
At first light, their small brown fingers grasp
a Pippin File, a skeleton key and they

looked up: Bramah winking! Her hands unlock
the doors Consortium sealed them in, blasted———

And did the aunties take the child, *yes they did, yes they did*
the doctor and the beggar girl, the mother and the son.

> *Jumped the fence*
> > *you should too.*

INSCRIBED ON THE WALLS OF MIGRANT CAMP #3

Those children—

Toxic Breeze!
Use your Sleeve!

Right as Rain
Good as New

Jumped the Fence
You Should Too

Roll Your Dice
Don't Think Twice

Un Coup de Dés
Jamais, Jamais

There's our Aunty Agatha!
Where's our Aunty Tabitha?

Hey, Bramah:
You R Our
English-
Masala Girl

Your Lock and Key
Will Set Us Free.

THE TALE OF THE VILLAGE SPY, FOUND IN THE YEAR 2087

Yes, they came for her, the woman named A.
No, of course I didn't get paid. Did my duty.

What? Well, she bloody well had it coming.
Never fails. Them righteous. Too smart for their own good.
Look at me. I've done all right, haven't I?
And look at our Betty then, just look at her!
Nothing wrong turning in a few words:
——Them with their stockholders' meetings
——I read things, too, you know.
——Betty, I says, *resistance is futile.*
Oh, we had a good laugh, just look at us.
Aren't I right, then? Everythings all bought and paid for.
Makes no difference in the end.

She should have bloody well just done the same,
if you ask me, what?

She cried out when they shaved her head then tarred
    that egg-fragile skull, her body whipped.
In the end she smiled her cracked lips and spoke

Lock and Key, soon you'll see
my body's gone; my boy's not dead.

Green and golden, never stolen
Bramah's drill will always open—

LAMENT OF THE STONE MARKER

>>>>>>

Up by the Wishing Well, winnowing stone
dark engravings, drill driver, un/known.

Here might lie one Abigail Anderson
*   (adopted) daughter, 2050–2087*
of Dr. A.E. Anderson, 2020–2057

RELINQUISHED AT THE GATE

Whetstone, knife and sword,
scissor, shears, one plough,
a scythe, with several markings,
to be investigated.

One night, the one inside the other:
Raphael, sang-spoke his dying mother,
she of the Tabby and Twill.
Warp, to stand, she'd tell him
a warning, *weft, to sleep,*
side by side—*Come oh Bramah
and save my child.*

Consortium: in the hours after
Abigail as alabaster, stone cold.
Raphael long gone, howling in the arms
of those four aunties who fled to the farm.

At the Gate of the Unlucky

THE ORACLE OF GOLD AND GREEN

Didn't I tell them then,
portal to portal, winter, spring and fall,
by the ferry to the Island
    round the campfire at midnight
candles left to burn, didn't I call them, then
    azure light, no real darkness and told them,
        Come Midsummer's Eve.
    Didn't I show them, then,
up at the farmhouse
    high in the loft
messages sent
    bird by bird: winter, spring and fall,
Beggar Boys with brooms, to sweep and to sing
Sword Girls to strike, sharp skilled, long limbed,
    each marked to bring,
A. to meet B. and all the As after,
always an Aunt Agatha
    and with her, Aunt Tabitha
    at every birth, a story to say:

Us on the farm, us by the river
bring us the gold, keep green forever
    were we to stand under moonlight so bright,
    our faces shimmering, silver at night
    right round our necks, three ribbons of red
    never forget us, even when we're dead.

Didn't I tell them, then, didn't I?
when the Tilt comes, all seasons will end.

VILLAGE WOMEN GOSSIP

There's our cousin Abigail lost in time.
She rode a white horse to a far field.
Men in the village cut out her tongue
they tarred and they feathered her coal-black hair.
Bald as an eagle she yet rides a white horse.

There's our sister Ellen, always in prison.
She's locked away in a mean little house
Whipped and silent as a dead mouse.
All her lives gathered and one day shot dead.

There's our Aunty Agatha. Her broken heart.
All her men short a dollar, all of them late.
There's our Aunty Tabitha. She's real old,
Her husband died early; he took all her gold.
Who'll ever tell that he fell down a well.

There's our Aunty Magda, river to mud,
her husband did drown, he fell with a thud
blown to bits by bombs, embraced by the sea
whenever we're asked, we say, *Don't look at me.*

Out by the well, there's a story to tell
there's a gun rusted over, there's roses and clover.
From womb to gate from Bramah to Fate—
One for the locket one for the key
One for the mountains and one for the sea.

FOUR AUNTIES AT THE WISHING WELL

Said Aunty Agatha:
Oh was there ever a tale of more woe.

Said Aunty Tabitha:
Than this our Abigail and all her foes?

Said Aunty Magda, the River Dweller:
As ye reap then you'll sow, elm to stone.

Said Aunty Maria, her beehives lost:
Find the skep, then you'll find the long way home.

Said they all together:
We've washed you in the Wishing Well
From Abigail Ellen to Abigail
Born or adopted, we'll never tell.

Said they all together:
Mother of the Forest, branched to be brave
They've stolen your acorns and we're forlorn
Your roots still embrace us, still we are here———
Bring us steel scissors, bring us silken threads
They've stolen your acorns, soon they'll be dead.

They looked up then, to see Bramah and a Beggar Boy———

OUTSIDE PERIMETER, FAINT ECHOES HEARD

A handful of children, pebbles in hand:

Abigail, Abigail, make no mistake
Faster and faster, you'll end at the Gate——

Who was your mother, we'll never tell
Who was your lover, some knew him well

Abigail, Abigail, shape-shifter, too
From Portal to Portal, you'll always be true.

Right as rain
Good as new

Jumped the fence
You should too!

THE BEGGAR BOY'S SONG

As Written by an Itinerant Scribe

Pay me a Penny
I'll sing you many:

Which oak box
This oak box

This Chalice
Is Without Malice

Right as Rain
Good as New

Jumped the Fence
You Should Too.

My mother named me.
Then she saved me.

Green and golden—
Raphael.

>>>>>>
♕ ♕ ♕

⋨

A Note to the Reader

Thank you for entering the world of THOT J BAP. I thought you might like to know a little bit more about this world and why I created it.

I was born in India in the city once known as Poona, an old British hill station about eight hundred kilometres north of Mumbai/Bombay. At the age of six months, I arrived in Canada via Gander, Newfoundland and then trekked with my family across the continent, coast to coast. We moved from St. John's up to St. Anthony, Labrador, then to Pictou County, Nova Scotia. From there we moved to Montreal, and then on to small-town Saskatchewan, finally settling down in the town of towns, New Westminster, British Columbia.

In grade school on the prairies and then in high school in British Columbia, I was, in those days, pretty much always the outsider, not really fitting in anywhere but eager to soak up the origin stories of other people, being rather embarrassed about my own: my father grew up a Hindu, my mother a Sunni Muslim, and they converted to Christianity. In fact, my father was one of the first South Asians ordained into the United Church of Canada as a graduate of McGill's Faculty of Divinity. In those days, in this settler country, if you said, "United Church" you were as "Canadian" as Timothy Eaton or *The Globe and Mail* or even, if on the fringes, the NDP.

Everywhere we lived, I was asked, "What kind of Indian are you?" Once, when my parents were teachers up in the border country between northern Quebec and northern Ontario, I played with my friend Roxanne. She broke the news to me that no, I could not attend her potlatch. I cried later, telling my mother who looked at me and said, "We're not that kind of Indian." She explained we didn't have any right to Roxanne's stories. I remember how quiet we both were, that faraway afternoon. We lived then in teachers' housing on the edge of the bay.

Now, as I write to you this winter of our pandemic in the year 2020, I think on these memories and share them with a sense of gratitude: that, as an immigrant-settler-citizen, I've been allowed to live here on the lands of others, soaking up Story, alive to the way Place whispers layers of secrets, about time and those eternal questions:

Where are you from? Who are your people?

I've always seen myself on the outside of those questions, searching for the answers that perhaps will be found in this book you hold in your hands.

Maybe one day you will find yourself asked about your story, all the *whys* and *wherefores*. Maybe then you'll think back on Bramah and her world, and when they ask you why—why portals, why gates, why rhymes?—you will heed the call of the four aunties of the Wishing Well. Maybe you will look around and see that cedar on the hill, rain running down its limbs, mist lowering the sky. And you will say to those who ask, *Go stand there. Wait.*

New Year's Eve, 2020

Name	Birth	Death	Age at Death
Dr. A.E. Anderson	2020	2057	37
Abigail	2050	2087	37
Bartholomew	2050	protected data	
Raphael	2084	unknown	
Aunty Agatha	1990	2130	140
Aunty Tabitha	1995	unknown	unknown
Aunty Maria	unknown	still alive	
Aunty Magda	unknown	still alive	

The INVESTIGATOR	protected data
Guards of the Fifth Gate	unavailable
Beggar Boys	undocumented
Sword Girls	sworn to secrecy

Bramah is a demigoddess/locksmith, unaware of her origins.

Mythic characters found in the tales told by Bramah's Grandmother:
Bloody-Eyed Jim, the Girl with a Thousand Pockets, Jai-Ishmael.

Throughout the world of THOT J BAP, we encounter a set of symbols that allude to the game of chess, to bio-contagion and viruses, to bees and to chemistry. Visit thotjbap.com, click on the key and use the code "2020" for more information about this epic.

Part One

In the far future, we meet Bramah, the locksmith summoned to do a job for Consortium. With Bramah is a Beggar Boy whom she befriends. Through a series of adventures they learn of an oak box at a farmhouse controlled by Consortium. Bramah is called to the farmhouse to unlock the oak box. She does this but also outwits the Guards and steals the box. Inside the box, Bramah and the Beggar Boy find many things, including an ancient parchment scroll. They read the scroll and the stories it contains of Aunty Maria, a Seed Saver who helps a group of outlawed scientists, including Dr. A.E. Anderson. We learn of the doctor's connection to the Women of the Wishing Well, including Aunty Agatha.

Before Dr. Anderson is incarcerated by Consortium and made a prisoner of the INVESTIGATOR, she helps a band of beggar children. She adopts one of them, a little girl, whom Aunty Agatha rescues, some say with the help of Bramah.

Part Two

This is the story of Abigail, the adopted daughter of Dr. A.E. Anderson, and takes place in the years 2057–2087. Abigail is brought up by Aunty Agatha who schools her in the healing arts and tells her stories of the Before-Time. Abigail journeys to the Great Cities of Transaction including Paris, Ahmedabad, Baghdad and finally chooses to heed her dead mother's wish: she becomes a Portal traveller and joins the resisters in their quest to save seeds and battle Consortium. Abigail meets the scholar Bartholomew. They fall in love, conceive a child and are imprisoned. Abigail gives birth to their son, Raphael.

CHRONOLOGY OF MAJOR EVENTS IN THOT J BAP: BOOK ONE

2020: the birth of Dr. A.E. Anderson during a bio-contagion.

2030–2050: a series of five eco-catastrophes leading to a world controlled by Consortium.

2050: the Battle of Kingsway.

2057: the worsening of planetary conditions that impact the lives of Abigail, adopted daughter of Dr. A.E. Anderson, and the Women of the Wishing Well.

2072: the Resisters continue to battle Consortium.

2087: the New Dark Ages.

The Far Future: where we first meet Bramah and the Beggar Boy.

A NOTE ON TIME TRAVEL IN THOT J BAP

In the world of THOT J BAP, time travel consists of observation only, like watching a hologram or a movie. Time travel is reserved for Certified Travellers, most of whom are on hire to Consortium, usually hunting down resisters. Bramah is a Certified Traveller and finds ways to subvert the terms of her contract to help others. Sometimes, Travellers will fall down Portals, by accident or due to evil forces.

I was born in the time of floods: forehead,
anointed with honey, brown skin glistening.

My first memories of poetry are the sounds of my father's gentle voice, English inflected with his mother tongue, Marathi, as he read me Mother Goose nursery rhymes. And later, the sound of my mother's voice singing in the basement, a sweet lilting Gujarati, her first language. My parents brought my sister and I up in the English of what I sometimes think of as "middle Canadiana." Not until 2010, as I worked on my first book and met the poet Marlene Nourbese Philip, did I develop a means to interrogate my "slipped tongue" and the pain-complexity of working in the only language I know, this conquistador, English.

Over the ten years I've spent working on this epic, THOT J BAP, I've been influenced by these reflections and hundreds of texts, including T.S. Eliot's *Four Quartets* and *The Wasteland*; Robin Blaser's collected works, *The Holy Forest*; Rachel Blau DuPlessis' *Drafts*; the poems and plays of Bertolt Brecht; and many editions of the work known as *The Arabian Nights*.

Add to these my lifelong companions Virgil, Dante, Chaucer, Shakespeare, Milton, plus translations of Homer's *Odyssey*, Wikipedia forays into Vedic scriptures, family gossip about Hindu gods, as well as rereadings of Christina Rossetti, Octavia Butler and an old red hymnal. Layered into all of that, readings of scientific reports on climate change and government malfeasance (CIA torture report) and many more documents, including the history of locksmithing, manuals on craft-making, old instruction books on inventions, out-of-date primers on astronomy, and even recordings of the late Robert Fisk as he spoke of world events in front of hundreds in a cathedral in downtown Vancouver.

And I've brought all of it into my obsession with formal poetry and with what I call docu-poetics, the breaking apart of text to create new forms, often in combination with visuals, such as symbols and signs.

This obsession finds its creative tension in the investigation of the fragment fused into forms of poetry such as blank verse, the sonnet, the madrigal, the ballad, not to mention, spells, codes and riddles. You'll find all these in THOT J BAP, plus new forms I've created and haven't yet named!

So there I was, working away with all this, and then our pandemic happened. And this story grabbed my fingers and off we went deeper into that ultimate portal, myth and magic. The question is, will I ever return to Before? ♛

ACKNOWLEDGEMENTS

An excerpt from the poem "The Summons" appears on a face mask designed by Debbie Westergaard Tuepah, commissioned by the Surrey Art Gallery, available for purchase spring 2021.

Earlier versions of selected poems appeared in chapbooks published by Nous-zot Press and above/ground press as well as in these literary journals: *The Rusty Toque, Eleven Eleven, Tripwire* and *The Capilano Review*. With gratitude to the late Marthe Reed and the late Peter Culley.

Iterations of THOT J BAP poems appeared in an outdoor eco-installation by the artist Chris Turnbull, photographs of which can be seen here: https://thecanadaproject.wordpress.com/what-is-thecanadaproject/thot-j-bap-collaboration-with-chris-turnbull/

Earlier iterations of selected poems from *The Battle of Kingsway*, a chapbook published by above/ground press in 2017 (bpNichol Chapbook Award finalist), were set to music by Owen Underhill of the Turning Point Ensemble. Special thanks to rob mclennan.

Earlier versions of selected poems are also found in the chapbook *Extractions from THOT J BAP* from Nomados Literary Publishers (2017), with thanks to Meredith Quartermain.

Two earlier iterations of the Abigail sonnets also appeared in *Canadian Literature* 233 (summer 2017) with thanks to Stephen Collis and Catriona Strang.

An earlier version of the poem "Bramah Remembers a Lullaby" appeared on a greeting card commissioned by the Surrey Art Gallery.

Thanks to Nightwood Editions and Silas White for editing and publishing this work and for sharing in the vision of innovative poetry and beautifully made books.

Love and gratitude to my husband: he took the time, in a pandemic, to read all of this epic fantasy.

Gratitude to the independent publishers and literary journals of Canada for their continued support of long-form poetry.

DEDICATION

———for all the lives lived in my families, the Saklikars and the Patels, past, present and future, including my grandma, Miriam Patel, who I never met. And my grandma, Godavari Saklikar, who visited me when I was a little girl in Saskatchewan. Attar of roses!

———to the memory of my father teaching me Mother Goose nursery rhymes.

———to the memory of my mother singing Gujarati in the basement up at the home house.

———to my sister, *Fare Forward, Voyagers!*

>>>>>>
♛ ♛ ♛
⬡

>>>>>>
♛ ♛ ♛
⬡

>>>>>>
♛ ♛ ♛